Y0-BZZ-283

Melati Lum is an Australian, Malay, Chinese, Muslim Lawyer who has worked as a Crown Prosecutor, prosecuting serious criminal offences in the courts. She has previously worked for the United Nations in The Hague in the prosecution of war crimes that occurred in the former Yugoslavia. She currently lives in Adelaide, Australia with her family. This is her first novel for pre-teens.

Ayesha Dean

The Istanbul Intrigue

MELATI LUM

Melby Rose Publishing

Ayesha Dean

The Istanbul Intrigue

Published in 2016 by Melby Rose Publishing

Copyright © 2016 Melati Lum

All rights reserved.

No part of this book may be reproduced or transmitted in any form
in any manner whatsoever without written permission from the
Publisher except where permitted by law.

A CIP catalogue record for this book is available from the National
Library of Australia.

ISBN: 9780994460509

Cover illustration and design by Nuri Septina.

Melby Rose Publishing, Adelaide, Australia.

www.melatilum.com.au

Dedicated to the person inside you who loves solving mysteries, and eating Turkish kebabs. Sometimes at the same time...

CHAPTER ONE

Ayesha Dean watched her friend Sara haul her bright pink suitcase on top of the luggage conveyor belt at the airport check-in counter. Sara was part of an Australian-Lebanese Christian family and Ayesha grinned as she saw Sara squeeze her eyes shut and cross her fingers.

"Please let it be under 20 kilos, please let it be under 20 kilos..." Sara chanted. Thankfully, the digital scales at the counter read 19.4 kilograms. "Oh thank God!" exclaimed Sara.

Ayesha laughed, "You won't have any weight

1

left for all the shopping you plan to do!"

Sara groaned as this thought sank in. She stepped to the side as Ayesha checked in with no issues. The two girls were to meet their friend, Jess, on the other side of the security-check area. They had just finished their final year at high school and were travelling to Istanbul, Turkey. Ayesha had recently celebrated her eighteenth birthday.

When Ayesha's Uncle Dave mentioned that he had a work conference to attend in Istanbul, Ayesha jumped at the chance to accompany him. Luckily for Ayesha, Sara's father and Uncle Dave were partners in their international legal firm and were both attending the conference.

Ayesha and Sara convinced Jess to join them. She would be staying with them, so all that Jess had to do was gather enough funds for the airfare and a bit of spending money. The day of departure had finally arrived and the three girls were thrilled. It was to be their grand adventure!

Ayesha and Sara made their way to the security checkpoint. This morning Ayesha had chosen a pair of boots that she knew wouldn't "beep" as she went through the security gate. She was wearing a bright blue hijab done up in a turban-style with soft skinny jeans and an oversized knit that came halfway to her knees. She knew that her clothes would be comfortable for the long flight ahead.

Ayesha braced herself for the inevitable "random" bomb check. She was surprised to walk straight past the bomb-check security guard, and chuckled to herself as she saw that Sara had instead been stopped behind her. Sara rolled her eyes before looking up and noticing that the young security guard was actually quite handsome. Ayesha smiled as she caught Sara inconspicuously patting her luxurious dark hair into place before asking the guard where to put her bags.

As the guard examined Sara's bags, Ayesha

turned to see Jess's curly blonde head in the distance bouncing up and down trying to get her attention. Jess looked very excited and was waving her arms frantically as she came towards them.

"Oh my goodness! I couldn't wait for you guys to get here. You have to hurry, they're boarding soon and we still have to go through customs!" breathed Jess. "Ayesha, I bumped into your uncle. He said to tell you that he's on his way to the lounge and he'll come and see you on the plane. You shouldn't have agreed to fly with us in economy when you could have gone in business class with your uncle. You're crazy, Ayesha Dean!"

Just then, Ayesha heard a man shout out from about 50 metres away, "Hey! He's taken my bag!" Ayesha looked towards the man's voice and saw a large crowd of people walking in the general direction of the boarding gates. Most of them appeared to be in a hurry, and Ayesha remembered that she had recently heard an airport announcement that there had been a gate change. She noticed that one young man in the middle of the crowd appeared to keep looking behind him. Something about his demeanour made Ayesha think that he had something to hide. A little further ahead, Ayesha saw that the man who had shouted was pointing to the shifty-looking youth within the crowd. Suddenly the youth began to run away from the crowd, towards one of the airport's exits. Ayesha dropped her bags and ran to intercept him, as he was moving very quickly in her direction.

As he was about to run past her, Ayesha stuck her leg out at just the right moment to trip him, and the force of his momentum sent him flying a few feet into the air before he landed on his stomach with a thud on the ground. The bag he had been holding went skidding along the airport floor. Ayesha immediately placed her knee into his back and expertly manoeuvred his arm into a martial arts hold behind his back. Ayesha could see that the offender was only a young teenager of about fifteen. "Ow! Let me go!" he pleaded. "I was just playing a joke, I wasn't really gonna take anything!"

"You can tell that to the court mate," Ayesha said. "You know you really shouldn't be doing this type of thing."

In a few short moments, airport security relieved Ayesha of her burden. An officer from the Australian Federal Police took a statement from Ayesha as well as her details. She was thinking of becoming a detective one day, but wanted to do some study and experience travelling the world first. She loved learning martial arts and had been training in Tae Kwon Do since she was ten years old.

Ayesha returned to her friends after giving her statement to the police. Jess looked very concerned, "Are you alright Ayesh? That was so awesome!"

"Yeah, I loved that side kick, trip thing you did with your foot. Maybe I should start training too," Sara added as she tried to mimic Ayesha's tripping action with her foot.

Ayesha laughed, "Thanks guys. You know I'd love it if you started training with me!"

A short while later, Ayesha and her friends settled into their seats on the plane and were served small packets of rice crackers and cups of orange juice.

"This is so exciting!" exclaimed Jess. "I can't wait to see Istanbul. I hear they even have bits of Ancient Roman ruins lying around on the side of the road because there's just so many of them."

"Yeah, I'm mainly looking forward to all the delicious food!" Sara laughed. "But of course, beautiful buildings, culture, history and all of that…"

Ayesha added, "And how awesome that we can all go together! These are the best holiday plans ever!"

Ayesha, Sara and Jess had been friends since their first day at Gum Tree Grove High School, when they had been put together for a "getting to know you" session. Ayesha had worn her hijab to school for the first time and she had been feeling a little nervous about how people would treat her. Sara and Jess had commented on how gorgeous Ayesha looked and they all instantly hit it off. From that day, the friends shared countless good times and bad throughout high school. Ayesha loved Sara's fierce loyalty, and Jess's beautiful, caring nature. She knew that they always had her back and she just enjoyed hanging out with them.

Ayesha heard a little bell signalling that the seatbelt sign had been turned off. A few minutes later she looked up to see Uncle Dave walking towards her from the front of the plane. "How's it going back here, love?" he said. "Are you guys all comfortable?"

"Hi Day!" Ayesha responded happily using the pet name she always called her uncle. "Yes, all fantastic thanks. We've got our snacks and headphones. We're all ready for the next fourteen hours."

The travellers were going to stop in Dubai for a short transit before continuing on to Istanbul. It was going to be a long journey of almost 24 hours altogether.

"How's business class?" Ayesha asked her uncle.

Uncle Dave let out a chuckle, "I can't complain! It would have been nicer if we could have travelled together, but I guess you don't want your old uncle to cramp your style, eh?"

"No, we couldn't have that," Ayesha joked. "Go back to your caviar, Day! See you when we land." Uncle Dave laughed and gave Ayesha a kiss on the forehead. He said goodbye and gave a little wave to the girls before making his way back to his seat.

Ayesha relaxed back into her seat and said a small prayer of thanks for her uncle. From the time Ayesha could remember, Uncle Dave had raised her as his own daughter. Ayesha's parents had died when she was still a baby, and her parents had named Dave as Ayesha's guardian, as he was their closest relative in Australia.

Ayesha's father was born into an Australian family of English heritage and became a Muslim when he was in his early twenties. He met and fell in love with Ayesha's mother while he was travelling through her village in Indonesia. When Ayesha was born, her parents appointed David Dean, Ayesha's uncle on her father's side, as her guardian if they happened to pass away. It was Ayesha's parents' wish that she be brought up as a

Muslim, even though Dave himself was not a religious man.

Ayesha had a happy childhood with her uncle and aunt in a comfortable neighbourhood called Gum Tree Grove. Every weekend, Uncle Dave would drive Ayesha to the nearest mosque, where she would learn about Islam and learn to read the Quran. Meanwhile, Dave would wait patiently for Ayesha in the courtyard and chat with the caretaker, or do some reading of his own. Dave felt blessed to be named Ayesha's guardian and he regarded it as his obligation to fulfil his brother's wishes of raising Ayesha as a Muslim. Ayesha was so grateful for having Uncle Dave and Aunt Lily in her life, and couldn't think of any two people she would have preferred to raise her.

Ayesha opened her eyes on the plane and looked at her friends seated beside her. Sara was bopping her head to what looked like a Bollywood movie on the screen in front of her, while Jess was watching the movie *Frozen* for the tenth time and singing 'Let it go' under her breath. Every month or so, Jess would get a song in her head and wouldn't stop tormenting Ayesha and Sara with singing the same song over and over whenever she had the chance. 'Let it go' was Jess's song of the month.

Ayesha smiled and said a quick "*Alhamdulillah.*" She was so happy to be going on this trip with her uncle and best friends. She loved travelling and seeing new places, meeting new people and experiencing different things. Every time Ayesha got on a plane, she felt an exciting sense of anticipation. She wondered what hidden stories Istanbul might hold, and what mysteries would come her way. Ayesha couldn't wait to find out!

CHAPTER TWO

Once they landed in Istanbul, Ayesha and her friends caught a taxi to their hotel with Uncle Dave, who sat in the front passenger seat. The first few moments after they stepped outside of the airport were exhilarating to Ayesha. She felt the rush of being in a different country surrounded by people speaking a different language. This was the first time Ayesha and her friends had been to Istanbul, although Ayesha had wanted to visit the city for a long time.

As the taxi drove through the streets, Uncle

Dave pointed out the great bridge that connected the European side of Istanbul to its Asian side. The girls found it incredible that this ancient yet modern city spanned the two separate continents of Europe and Asia.

The taxi took the travellers to their hotel in the Sultanahmet area, which was the old historic part of the city. On the way there, the girls caught glimpses of the famous Blue Mosque that was built by the Ottoman Sultan Ahmet I in the seventeenth century. They craned their necks for a quick peek at the outside of the impressive Hagia Sophia. Uncle Dave smiled as the girls expressed delight at seeing the ancient structure. "Did you know that the Hagia Sophia was built as a church in the sixth century by Byzantine Emperor Justinian I?" he asked.

"Er, not all of us are as up to date on our history as you, Day," Ayesha responded. He laughed and began mimicking the monotone voice of a tour operator. "The building was later used as a mosque from the fifteenth century, but it was converted into a museum in 1935..."

Ayesha was very keen to get out and start exploring after glimpsing these beautiful old buildings from the taxi. She had read about the abundance of very old, grand libraries, monuments and mosques in this ancient city, and couldn't wait to find out more about its history and its people.

It was mid-morning by the time the group arrived at the hotel. They were staying at a beautiful, small boutique hotel in the middle of the old quarter of Istanbul, within walking distance from most of the main historic sites.

Sara's father, Mr Isa, had arrived at the hotel two days earlier in order to attend some early meetings before the business conference. He was waiting for them in the lobby when they arrived. Sara ran up to her father and kissed him on the cheek. He hugged her in return, "Welcome *habibti*! How was your flight?"

"Fine thanks Dad, I am so excited to be here!" Mr Isa laughed and said, "Make sure you guys stick together, OK? And avoid the carpet sellers. I don't want to be carrying a carpet back on the plane with me!"

The travellers made their way to the front desk where they met Mrs Nurhan, the owner of the hotel. Mrs Nurhan welcomed them to the hotel and provided them with keys to their rooms as well as maps of the city. She explained that it was very easy to get around the city using the local trams, and that the guests should call concierge if they needed anything that would make their stay more pleasant.

Uncle Dave and Mr Isa then caught up with each other to discuss what was happening with their business conference. They left the girls to do their own exploring. Earlier, Uncle Dave had checked to see that Ayesha had her phone with her, just in case she needed to call him.

Ayesha and her friends decided to have a quick look around the hotel before heading out to see the city sights. All the rooms of the hotel, including its small lobby, opened onto a quaint yet peaceful open-air courtyard. The courtyard was paved with a stunning cerulean-blue tiled mosaic. The middle of the courtyard housed a large clay water feature shaped like a vase, with rippling sounds that provided a calm ambience. Potted plants framed the sides of the courtyard and were placed near the doors to each of the rooms.

Each of the hotel rooms had a small kitchenette and a beautiful marble bathroom with modern facilities. The interior of the girls' room was decorated in a romantic style, reminiscent of the Ottoman era. Uncle Dave was staying in the room a few doors down from them, and Sara's father's room was also nearby. The breakfast room was located up a flight of stairs through the lobby, where Mrs Nurhan had said that the guests could look forward to enjoying a traditional Turkish breakfast each morning.

Ayesha and her friends burst into their hotel room with excitement. The neutral-coloured walls were decorated with paintings of the Turkish countryside, as well as scenes from the Ottoman Court in the era of the sultans. There were twin single beds to the right of the front door, and an extra single bed had been brought in to accommodate the third guest. The room was a comfortable size, but could not be described as overly spacious. The third bed had been placed near the foot of the two single beds, a few meters in front of the doorway. The kitchenette and bathroom were beyond the extra bed on the opposite side facing the front door. The beds were soft and comfortable, and had been made up with fresh, luxurious-looking white linen.

Jess immediately said, "I'll take the extra bed guys!" as she kicked her shoes off and jumped on the extra bed. Standing on her bed, Jess pretended she had a microphone in her hand and started singing, "Let it gooo, let it gooo! Can't hold it back anymore!"

"Aargh please stop! This has to be the thousandth time!" Sara cried as she held her hands over her ears. She then grabbed several cushions off her bed and started playfully throwing them at Jess, who merely ducked and kept on singing. Ayesha laughed at her friends and announced that she was going to see what goodies she could find in the bathroom. This got the attention of the other two and they all went to exclaim over the beautifully appointed marble bathroom together.

Once they were finally settled into their hotel room, the girls put their bags down and quickly freshened up. "Where shall we go first?" Ayesha asked, knowing what the answer would be.

"The Grand Bazaar!" shouted Sara and Jess at the same time.

***

Ayesha and her friends stepped off the tram into a crowded street that housed one of the main entrances to the famous Grand Bazaar of Istanbul. As the girls walked under the archway leading into the Grand Bazaar complex, Sara squealed with delight at all the open-air stalls that were just outside of the main building. "There's so much to choose from and we're not even inside the main section yet!"

The girls continued on towards the main section of the markets and passed under another large archway before finding themselves surrounded by thousands of stalls arranged in long aisles as far as the eye could see. The stalls were housed under a huge covered building designed with beautiful archways decorated with blue tiled mosaics.

Ayesha's eyes widened as she took in all of the different colours and the sheer volume of the various wares on display. From shoes to intricately embroidered cushion covers, coloured Turkish lamps, jewellery, clothing, carpets and scarves…it was as if Istanbul had tried to fit everything anyone could possibly want to buy under one large roof!

The girls spent a couple of pleasant hours searching the stalls for souvenirs and getting used to bargaining for everything they bought. With their new treasures, Ayesha suggested that they head to the Old Book Bazaar, which had been a book market since Byzantine times. She was hoping that she would be able to find Uncle Dave an extra special gift. She knew that he would really appreciate an antique book.

The Old Book Bazaar was located on one side of the Grand Bazaar and consisted of an open-air courtyard that was lined with small bookshops. Unlike most of the stalls inside the Grand Bazaar, many of these bookshops appeared to be separate little stores behind glass windows rather than open stalls. Tables had been set up outside each of the stores, displaying a variety of different second-hand books. Some of the books appeared to be very old, and others appeared to be novels or pre-owned books from more modern times.

Ayesha was more interested in searching for antique manuscripts. She saw a shop displaying what appeared to be a very old Quran underneath a glass cabinet in the front window. Ayesha let the others know she wanted to go inside.

The girls pushed open a glass door to enter the shop and a little bell rang from above to alert the owner that customers had come in. The shop had appeared quite small from outside, but once the girls entered, they could see that there was a doorway leading into a further room in which they could browse for more items.

The walls of the front room of the shop were lined with glass cabinets displaying antique books, Qurans, and various documents written in ancient Arabic script. The lighting was dim. Ayesha wondered if it was to protect the documents. There was a musty, not unpleasant, 'old book smell' in the air that reminded Ayesha of her childhood when she used to trawl through her local second-hand bookshop for bargains.

Less than a minute after the girls entered the bookshop, a short, smiling, Turkish man with a moustache came into the front room from somewhere at the back. *"Merhaba, Merhaba!* Welcome, Welcome! Come in!"* he said in a jolly manner.

Ayesha smiled, *"Tesekkuler,* thank you! I couldn't resist coming in when I saw that beautiful Quran displayed in the front window."

"Oh yes, it is very beautiful, is it not?" the man answered. "That one is from the seventeenth century and it is my favourite in this shop!"

Jess happily stated, "I am surprised at how many people speak English here. Of course, being a visitor to this city, I should have made an effort to learn some words in the local language, but it is quite easy to get around using English."

"Yes, yes," the smiling man said. "In this city, we rely much on tourism, so many people in the tourist area know some English…mine is not very good. I can improve, but my son has taught me a little bit."

"No, no, your English is excellent!" the girls exclaimed. The man chuckled and put his hand to his chest. "*Tesekkuler*. My name is Mehmet. What can I help you with today?"

Ayesha said, "I'm looking for a gift for my uncle. He likes antique maps, or anything antique really. I have a budget though, so I won't be able to spend too much money."

"OK," Mehmet said. "Well, you have come to the right place. Let us see what we can find."

Mehmet led the girls into the back room of the shop. The shelves of this room were filled with hundreds of old books and there were additional tables, cabinets and boxes on the ground. Every surface seemed to be overflowing with more books and papers.

"What time are you looking for?" Mehmet asked Ayesha. Ayesha noticed that the prices of some of the books displayed in the front room cost several thousand dollars. She knew that, generally, the older books would be more expensive, so she asked Mehmet to show her some items from within a fairly recent timeframe.

Mehmet led Ayesha to a large open box on the floor. "This box came yesterday. I looked at them and they are from the last hundred years. There is not anything very expensive in this box, but there are nice books."

Ayesha started browsing through the items in the box. It wasn't long before she came across the perfect gift for her uncle. It was a brown leather-bound book of printed maps. The maps themselves were not the originals, but the book contained dozens of prints of very old maps from hundreds of years ago. The leather cover of the book looked worn and faded, and the pages had become yellow with age. Ayesha knew that Uncle Dave would love it.

Ayesha bought the book and promised Mehmet that they would be back soon. They would be staying in Istanbul for ten days and it was so peaceful browsing in Mehmet's shop that Ayesha knew she would return to make a purchase for herself.

As they were about to leave, a tall, dark-haired, handsome young man entered the shop from the back door. Mehmet laughed, "Ah! Just in time, girls. Before you leave, please meet my son, Emre!"

Emre looked pointedly at his father, and then laughed and greeted the girls. "My Dad is always trying to match-make me with all of his female customers. He just called me in saying that there was an emergency at the shop! Well, at least this time you are all under fifty!"

Ayesha laughed good-naturedly. Emre looked about eighteen or nineteen years old. He had an easy-going, relaxed personality, and a friendly, open manner about him that appealed to her. He asked Ayesha where they were planning on going next, as he was on holidays and was happy to show them around.

Ayesha looked at her friends. They were both smiling and nodding. Ayesha looked at Mehmet. He too was smiling and nodding. "Oh well," Ayesha thought, "There are three of us girls, and at least I am a trained black belt if I ever need to use those skills."

Ayesha nodded and said, "OK great, let's go. Shall we go to the Blue Mosque?"

An hour or so later, Ayesha, her friends, and Emre were sitting in the beautiful gardens outside the Blue Mosque, enjoying some cakes that they had purchased from a roadside vendor. Jess, who was trying to eat more healthily, had refused the cakes and had found herself some delicious roadside corn-on-the-cob instead. They had just been inside the Blue Mosque and admired its impressive, intricately detailed domed ceilings. Ayesha had taken the opportunity to do her *Zuhr* and *Asr* afternoon prayers together in the mosque's inspirational setting. Emre had also said his prayers. Ayesha thought it was wonderful that the locals did their *salat* prayers in one of the country's most famous landmarks.

Relaxing with her friends in the gardens of the

Blue Mosque, Ayesha took the old book of maps out of her backpack to have another look at it. She loved the feeling of the old book in her hands, and the way the leather cover was worn at the edges. Ayesha thought that this book must have been used a lot and had been well loved to be as worn out as it was. She opened the cover and realised that she had opened the back cover this time. The front and back covers looked exactly the same.

Inside the back cover, Ayesha noticed something that she hadn't seen while she was in Mehmet's dimly lit shop. There was a slight bulge inside the back cover of the book. The old leather cover was stitched onto the book itself, and there did not appear to be any holes or pockets in the cover.

Running her finger along the edge of the inside seam of the book's binding, Ayesha could feel that the stitching along one edge of the book was different from the stitching along all the other edges. The stitching on this one side seemed irregular. Ayesha's detective mind went straight into gear. "Hmm, what do we have here?" she said to the others.

She passed the book to Sara, who unfortunately had just managed to get some jam from the cake all over her top lip. Sara wiped her hands and face on a napkin and laughed, "Great timing!" She then ran her fingers along the stitched edge where Ayesha had indicated.

"It seems that the stitching along this edge is not very professionally done," Sara observed.

Jess piped up, "What are you thinking Ayesha? Shall we do a bit of unpicking?"

Emre said incredulously, "I thought you said this was a present for your uncle?"

Ayesha said, "Yes it is, but how could I just ignore a mysterious bulge in a beautiful old book?" She opened her eyes wide. "Sara is excellent at stitching and can patch it up when we get back to the hotel, right Sara?"

"Well," Sara said, as she felt along the edge of the book's seam again. "If this is the standard of stitching you are after, I can at least get it back to this standard. It's not very well done."

Ayesha felt her way along the book's seam for the loosest stitch. From her tote bag she took the travel-sized sewing kit that she had found in their hotel room. It contained a tiny pair of sewing scissors. As Ayesha used the scissors to loosen and cut the irregular stitching on the back cover, Jess laughed. "Ayesha you are always prepared for anything with that bag of yours!"

Ayesha finally loosened all of the stitching on the top side of the back cover. She slipped her hand inside the pocket that had been created and pulled out a thick piece of folded paper. Ayesha gave a small gasp as she opened the paper. It was a hidden note!

CHAPTER THREE

Ayesha examined the note in her hand. She noticed that the paper appeared to be a little dusty, but it was still white and did not appear to be very old. The others leaned in closer to see what it was. They were all tense with anticipation. "What does the note say?" asked Sara excitedly.

"It's in Turkish," said Ayesha. "Perhaps Emre can translate it for us."

Ayesha passed the note to Emre, who translated it and read out the English for them: *"To my dear Friend,*

If you have found this note, it means I am no longer in this life.

The Seven are not lost.

They are hidden for their own protection.

They belong together in the Suleymaniye Kutuphanesi but the time is not right.

I pray that you are true, and that your heart is clear.

What you seek contains the knowledge of the Shaykh al-Akbar.

Within the forbidden place.

Become one with the mirror.

Look beyond it to find your heart's desire.

I pray that you can return The Seven to their resting place.

May Allah be with you."

Emre finished translating the note and said, "It is signed, '*B.Ev*'. Hmm that is strange. Ev is not really a common Turkish surname."

"Does it mean anything?" asked Ayesha.

"Well, it usually means 'home' or 'house', but I guess it could also be a last name," he shrugged.

Ayesha looked at her friends in excitement. "A mystery to be solved! I wonder who the Shaykh al-Akbar is? Maybe Uncle Dave will know. They should be finished with their conference for the day by now!"

Ayesha asked Emre if he could write the English translation next to each line in the note. After he had done so, the girls said goodbye to him as they planned to head back to their hotel. Emre told them that the Suleymaniye Kutuphanesi was the old Suleymaniye Library, which was easy to get to by tram from their hotel. He said that he would be working in his father's shop for the next few days and he hoped that they would visit him there. He was also curious about the secret note, and told Ayesha that he would try to find out from his father where the book had come from.

Before he left, Emre looked at Ayesha and smiled, "Now I *know* that I will see you again as I may have more information that you can squeeze out of me."

Ayesha laughed, "I *would* be really grateful for any information you can find out about who brought that book into your dad's shop…and we'd like to see you again for sure!"

Back at the hotel, Ayesha and her friends met up with Uncle Dave and Mr Isa for dinner in the hotel restaurant. They were served a delicious array of Turkish foods including spinach and cheese *pide*, a baked, tasty, meat and vegetable dish called *karniyarik*, fluffy white rice, fresh hot bread and succulent Turkish salads.

Once the group had started their meal, Ayesha addressed Uncle Dave. "Day, today I bought you a gift, but I can't really give it to you yet because…we need it to solve a mystery."

"Ah, I wouldn't want to get in the way of another one of your mysteries Ayesha! You know that," Uncle Dave exclaimed. "What's the mystery this time?"

Ayesha grinned, "We found a note that was hidden inside an old book, which is eventually going to be your gift, by the way." She took the hidden note out of her pocket and handed it to her uncle. "Do you have any idea who the Shaykh al-Akbar is?"

"Hmm," Uncle Dave perused Emre's translation of the note. "Shaykh al-Akbar is what they call one of the greatest Sufi masters of the twelfth century, Ibn Arabi. He was also called 'The Great Shaykh.' I have just started reading about him. As you know, I'm interested in Sufism. It's fascinating. Apparently he wrote many hundreds of works and perhaps not all of the manuscripts have yet been discovered."

"I guess that any manuscript written by Ibn Arabi would be worth a lot of money?" Ayesha asked.

"Oh yes, of course," continued Uncle Dave. "Some antique manuscripts, not only those of Ibn Arabi but other famous scholars too, have been known to fetch hundreds of thousands of dollars at auction. I've heard that some of the rarer manuscripts have been stolen from the homes of old families who have passed them down through the generations. It's thought that many stolen manuscripts have been sold on the black market."

Jess spoke up, "Do you think that's why the person wrote the note? Because they were worried that someone would steal some manuscripts?"

"Perhaps," said Ayesha. "The note refers to the knowledge of the Shaykh al-Akbar. That could be referring to his manuscripts. But what manuscripts are we looking for, and where are they?"

Uncle Dave finished chewing on a succulent piece of doner kebab. "Ayesha, whatever you do, please tread carefully. Rare manuscripts are taken very seriously by all sorts of people, as they should be, but unfortunately the lure of money can attract some very unsavoury characters."

Ayesha agreed with her uncle, but could not get the mystery out of her mind for the rest of the meal.

***

The next day, Ayesha and her two friends caught the tram to the Suleymaniye complex, which housed the Suleymaniye Library. Ayesha lent her friends spare hijabs to drape over their heads while they visited the majestic Suleymaniye Mosque, built in the sixteenth century on the orders of Sultan Suleyman, also known as Suleyman the Magnificent. Ayesha herself was wearing a shiny turquoise coloured hijab arranged in a simple traditional Turkish style with one piece of the material pinned up behind her head. Today Ayesha had teamed her hijab with black skinny jeans, ankle boots, and a fitted white linen shirt-dress.

As she entered the vast courtyard in front of the entrance to the mosque, Ayesha felt a keen sense of peace as she imagined this same courtyard being used 400 years ago by worshippers on their way to prayer. Ayesha thought that the lovely thing about visiting this impressive ancient monument was that it was still a working mosque. She left Jess and Sara, who were happily looking around the courtyard, to quickly do her prayers under the main dome of the mosque.

A short time later, Ayesha and her friends found their way to the Suleymaniye Library. The library was located on the site where two *medressas,* or schools, were originally built in the sixteenth century as part of the mosque complex commissioned by Sultan Suleyman.

The library was not busy. There were some university students studying here and there, and some older, Ayesha thought, 'scholarly-looking' people around, but the peaceful space was not crowded.

At the information desk sat an attractive and friendly-looking woman of about thirty, who wore glasses and had her pastel pink hijab tied back behind her neck. The woman spoke English with a slight Turkish accent. "Welcome to the Suleymaniye Kutuphanesi, my name is Emina. May I help you?"

Ayesha introduced herself and her friends and asked if she could speak to the head librarian.

"Why yes! That is me," replied Emina. "My father was the head librarian for many years, but he has recently fallen ill and I have taken his place. I think there must be nobody in Istanbul who loves this place more than me. I have been coming here with my father since I was a child and he taught me everything he knows."

Emina made the girls feel welcome with her warm smile and friendly manner. It was obvious to

Ayesha that Emina was passionate about her job and genuinely loved the library.

Ayesha began, "We were wondering whether any Ibn Arabi manuscripts can be found in this library?"

Emina's face lit up at the mention of Ibn Arabi, "Oh yes, we have many works by Ibn Arabi in this library. We scan the original works. The digitised copies can be seen on our computers. This is so that the originals can be preserved."

"What a great project!" Ayesha exclaimed. "Just out of interest, may I also ask how the library got these manuscripts?"

Emina proudly replied, "The Suleymaniye complex has housed libraries since it was built in the sixteenth century. But today our library is the largest manuscript library in Turkey. We have one of the largest collections of Islamic manuscripts in the world."

Emina continued, "Many of the manuscripts have

come from other mosques and *medressas* over the years. A lot have also been donated from private citizens, and some have been held in families for generations."

Ayesha asked, "Do you know of any Ibn Arabi manuscripts that may have gone missing in the past?"

Emina looked thoughtful, "Well, we try our best to locate any manuscripts that are of public value, but it is not possible to know of every manuscript that may be out there. Although…" Emina paused, "I do remember my father once talking about some manuscripts he was hoping to acquire for the library a few years ago. They were not original works of Ibn Arabi, but I recall that they might have been some very valuable copies of one of his works by one of his close disciples. My father never got to see the manuscripts. Unfortunately my father had some sort of disagreement with the donor and we never saw the donor again."

Sara exclaimed, "The donor could be the person who wrote the note we found in the book!"

"What book?" asked Emina.

Ayesha explained, "I bought a book from the Old Book Bazaar…"

"It was such a wonderful shop!" Jess added.

"Oh! You must have been to see Mehmet?" Emina smiled. "He has an excellent collection."

"Yes," Ayesha agreed. She directed the conversation back to the donor. "Emina, did you know the name of the donor who wanted to donate those manuscripts? Did you ever meet him?"

Emina replied sadly, "No, unfortunately I did not know his name, and when I asked my father about him later, he did not want to talk about it. I'm not sure why. It seemed to upset my father so I never asked him about the man again. I had the feeling that they must have been friends in the past."

Ayesha responded, "What a shame. Oh well, I was just interested in finding out a bit more about Ibn Arabi. Can you please show me where I can do a manuscript search?"

"Of course!" Emina exclaimed.

As Ayesha turned around to follow Emina into the next room, she saw a gaunt-looking, middle-aged man with a skinny brown goatee, standing nearby and staring at her with an intense look in his eye. Ayesha had not noticed that he had been quietly putting some books away in the corner shelf behind them.

Feeling his beady eyes studying her as she walked past him, Ayesha felt a cold shiver along her spine. It appeared to Ayesha that the man had been secretly listening to their conversation!

CHAPTER FOUR

As Emina lead the girls towards the computer room, the man lowered his eyes and continued stacking books on the shelves. Emina spoke to the man as she passed him in a subdued voice, "Berke, can you please answer the telephone if it rings?"

The man nodded and continued with his task. Ayesha relaxed. "Oh, he works here," she thought. "I guess I shouldn't automatically think *everyone* is interested in what I'm doing." Ayesha silently laughed at herself. "He's harmless," she thought as they left him behind.

The interior of the computer room appeared quite modern, even though it was located in a very old building. The room had recently been refurbished and contained numerous computer work stations. Emina showed Ayesha to a computer and taught her how to use the library database search system.

Before she started her research, Ayesha turned to her friends and suggested that she was happy to do a bit of research on her own if they wanted to do a bit of sight-seeing instead. They agreed, as there was an art gallery around the corner that Sara and Jess really wanted to visit. The friends arranged to meet up in a couple of hours for lunch.

Ayesha spent the next half an hour on the computer writing down lists of Ibn Arabi publications that were available in the library. She also noted the details of where she could find the publications within the library.

Ayesha learnt that Ibn Arabi had written a piece of work that was known by several different names, one of the titles being *Awrad-al-Usbu*, or "Prayers for the Week". Another translation of the same title was, "The Seven Days of the Heart-Prayers for the Nights and Days of the Week." Each translated title for this same work had some mention of the concept of "days".

Ayesha's heart quickened as she read that the *Awrad-al-Usbu* comprised fourteen prayers, each one devoted to a particular day or night of the week. The prayers appeared to be personal prayers of Ibn Arabi, expressing an intimate conversation with his Beloved Creator, Allah. Ayesha noted that Ibn Arabi considered the seven days of the week to be sacred, and a divine sign from Allah pointing to the "Reality of Being" or "Existence".

"Wow, this is heavy," Ayesha thought as she learnt more about the *Awrad-al Usbu*. "I'm definitely going to try and learn more about this amazing scholar. But for now, I need to find out exactly what I should be looking for!"

Ayesha took a piece of paper out of her bag and wrote down the aisle and reference number for where she could locate copies of the *Awrad-al-Usbu* in the library. She then picked up her bag and made her way downstairs to the archive section.

Once she was downstairs, Ayesha immediately noticed that everything seemed a lot quieter and less busy than it was in the computer room. In the archive section below, Ayesha observed a large room with rows and rows of books arranged on numerous aisles of shelves. Each aisle was labelled with a letter and a number from one to three, so she could see that there were aisles labelled A1, A2, A3, B1, B2, B3 and so on.

Near the entrance to the archive room, Ayesha saw some seats that were empty. She noticed that nobody was around. Ayesha thought, "It's no wonder nobody is down here reading, the lights are so dim you could hardly read what was on your page."

Ayesha looked at the piece of paper telling her where to find an English translation of Ibn Arabi's *Awrad-al-Usbu*. She glanced at her notepaper where she had written "T3", and walked deeper into the dark archive section towards the back of the large room. The heels of Ayesha's boots echoed as she walked on the hard flooring. She peeked into each aisle as she passed, to see if there was anybody in this deserted section of the library. "Uncle Dave warned me about being in isolated places," she reminded herself. "It's always good to be aware of your surroundings." She didn't see any people downstairs at all.

After spending some time searching the numbers on the shelves, Ayesha found the section where several of Ibn Arabi's works were located.

Ayesha picked up a copy of *The Seven Days of the Heart* and began reading. She thought perhaps she could find a clue, or inspiration on what she should be searching for. Once she picked up the book, Ayesha became so absorbed in the beauty of what she was reading that she forgot where she was.

After some time, Ayesha felt an uncomfortable, prickly feeling on the back of her neck. She had the uneasy sensation that she was being watched. Ayesha stilled, and was suddenly very aware of her isolated, dimly lit surroundings. While she continued to look down at her book, Ayesha noticed a slight shadow pass over the page she was reading.

She turned around rapidly and gasped in shock. A man was standing about one metre behind her. She didn't know how long he had been there. He must have walked up to her very softly because she didn't hear him coming at all. She looked at his grey, thin face and recognised Berke, the librarian who had been stacking shelves earlier. He was staring intensely at her now, and quickly spoke in a creaky, low-pitched voice. "I'm sorry to have startled you. Ayesha, isn't it?"

He took a step closer. Ayesha instinctively took a quick step back. He continued unfazed. "I couldn't help overhearing your conversation with Emina earlier. And I noticed that you were searching on the computer for the *Awrad-al-Usbu*. Why are you so interested? What are you searching for?"

Keeping a close watch on the man's movements, Ayesha started to manoeuvre herself closer to the end of the aisle, which was nearer to the exit. She responded, "I don't think it is any of your business what my interests are. I could ask you the same thing. Why are you so interested?"

The man bowed his head towards her. "Again, I am sorry to have startled you. I am merely a librarian trying to help you."

Ayesha quickly moved past Berke who had been partially blocking her way out. Once she passed him she ran towards the exit and called back over her shoulder. "Thank you for your concern, but I think I can manage without your help."

Once she was back upstairs, Ayesha heard the sound of other people moving around the library. She breathed a sigh of relief. "Woah, that man gives me the creeps," she thought. "My instinct was right the first time I saw him."

Ayesha wondered, "Why was he so interested in what I was researching? Was he honestly just trying to be a helpful librarian? Did he know something about the *Awrad-al-Usbu* that might relate to the mysterious note?"

Ayesha shivered, remembering the prickly feeling she felt just before she turned around to find Berke staring at her. She thought, "Why on earth did he have to be so creepy about it all?!"

***

With the English translation of *The Seven Days of the Heart* still in her hand, Ayesha made her way to the front desk to speak with Emina again. After all her research, Ayesha still didn't know what she was looking for. Perhaps Emina could give her some ideas.

Emina smiled when she saw Ayesha with a book in her hand. "Did you find what you were looking for?" she asked.

"Kind of, but not really," Ayesha replied. "Emina, this may sound like a weird question, but may I speak with you in private? I think you may be able to help me, but I'd prefer to keep our conversation confidential."

Emina looked concerned, "Of course. I will just get someone to look after the desk and we will move to another room. I am always happy to help someone in need."

Emina lead Ayesha into a private office, and they sat down at a cosy table with a pot of tea between them. Ayesha was enjoying the sweet and subtle taste of this tea, which was so different from the plain tea she was used to drinking at home. She thought she could detect a hint of spice in the Turkish tea, which she found comforting and pleasantly uplifting.

"Thank you so much for the tea," Ayesha smiled. "It's just what I need right now."

Emina smiled back, "It is my pleasure. I don't often have the chance to share a cup of tea anymore, now that my father is so ill. I spend nearly every waking hour here in the library or looking after him. So it is good just to sit and have a chat for a while."

Ayesha found that she had a really nice, positive feeling around Emina. She thought that if Emina lived in Australia, they would be good friends. Ayesha couldn't help asking, "Do you have any other family, or perhaps, a…significant other person in your life?"

Emina laughed, "No! No husband, or fiancé to complicate my life at the moment. I'm not in a hurry. If someone special comes my way then so be it. Otherwise I am still single and free," she smiled.

"Oh, me too!" Ayesha responded, "I love being single and free. For now."

They both laughed.

"So," Emina got down to business. "How can I help you?"

Ayesha felt that Emina could be trusted, but her recent experience with Berke, the creepy librarian, made her cautious. She tentatively asked, "Your librarian Berke…er…do you know him well?"

Emina replied matter-of-factly. "He has been at the library for a couple of months now. I do not know him that well, but he seems to do his job. He usually keeps to himself and does not talk much. Why, has he done something I should be aware of?"

"No, no," Ayesha responded quickly. "I just wondered. He was asking me about my research and seemed rather insistent. That's all. Nothing to be reported."

Ayesha secretly thought, "Nothing yet. Hopefully it stays that way. I had better watch out for him."

She then asked, "Can you tell me anything about the manuscripts of Ibn Arabi's, *Awrad-al-Usbu?* Are all the original manuscripts accounted for?"

Emina paused and looked thoughtfully at Ayesha. "Is this the reason why you wanted to speak in private? If so, I can understand why."

Ayesha raised her eyebrows and replied, "Can you tell me anything about this book? Why did you say that you understand my concern for privacy?"

Emina nodded, "The original manuscripts are accounted for, but during the time of Ibn Arabi in the twelfth century and some time after that, many of his disciples copied his works and often wrote their own works commenting on and analysing the work of the Great Shaykh. It is thought that one of Ibn Arabi's close disciples made a beautifully intricate copy of the *Awrad-al-Usbu,* or what has been called *The Seven Days of the Heart.* This manuscript is said to be decorated with swathes of gold-leaf detail and rare coloured patterns in the borders of the pages. It is said to be a beautiful and impressive copy of the original *Awrad-al-Usbu* and as the copy is from the twelfth century, the manuscript is now worth a lot of money."

Ayesha's ears pricked up as she listened to what Emina had to say. She couldn't stop the thoughts from rushing through her head, "Twelfth century manuscript. The *Awrad-al-Usbu,* or *The Seven Days of the Heart.* Ibn Arabi, the knowledge of the Shaykh al-Akbar…"

Ayesha felt the excitement building. She wondered if the manuscript Emina was describing could be 'The Seven' that was mentioned in the hidden note!

CHAPTER FIVE

Ayesha controlled the urge to interrupt as she listened to Emina continue. "My father once told me that whoever found the lost manuscript of the *Awrad-al-Usbu* would either be a hero to the cause of public knowledge and appreciation, or a very, very rich villain who had lost their soul." Emina smiled, "My father can be a bit dramatic at times."

Ayesha asked, "So this manuscript was lost? What happened?"

Emina replied, "Actually, we are not sure

whether it was lost, or whether it still even exists. It is something of a fabled manuscript among the Librarians due to its artistic beauty and historical significance."

Emina sighed and sat back in her chair. "My father and I are part of a group of librarians who are devoted to the preservation of significant Islamic manuscripts. We call ourselves the Librarians and our group has been in existence for hundreds of years. I realise it is not the most original of names, but historically, all respectable librarians from the major libraries throughout the Islamic lands were part of the organisation. In modern times, only those of us who have a strong interest in historic manuscripts make an effort to remain part of the group. However, there are so many members of the Librarians around the world these days that the group has lost its exclusivity. In the past, to become a member, a person would have to pass a number of difficult tests and knowledge requirements. These days you just need to work in a library, register your details with the organisation, and pay a yearly membership fee."

Emina continued, "Anyway, according to the story that has been passed around the Librarians, this manuscript has been owned by many people over many generations. Many of the other manuscripts were passed down from one generation to the next. However, this manuscript was not necessarily held by the same family. Instead, whoever held the manuscript would choose the most reliable, trustworthy person who would be the next 'Keeper' of the manuscript after them."

"It makes sense that a Keeper would choose someone trustworthy to look after the manuscript," Ayesha said. "I guess the Keepers could not always trust a member of their own family to do the right thing."

"Exactly," Emina agreed. "But there is no guarantee that each Keeper would have made the best decision either." She continued, "In the past, the Librarians always kept an eye on who was the current Keeper of the manuscript. So the Librarians provided another safeguard for the manuscript with their knowledge of its whereabouts."

Emina took another sip of tea before continuing her story, "About one hundred years ago, according to my father, the Librarians lost track of who was holding the manuscript. For some reason or another, the Keeper of the manuscript did not want the Librarians to know who held it anymore, and the communication that had existed between the Keepers of the manuscript and the Librarians for so long, died out."

Emina took a breath, "So since the Keepers stopped talking, we Librarians have lost track of what became of the beautiful manuscript. Who knows? It may now be destroyed or lost and we have no idea. It is such a shame."

Emina threw a questioning look at Ayesha, "Can you tell me why you are interested in all of this?"

Ayesha considered her response. "I'm trying to solve a mystery, and what you've told me has been very helpful. I can't really say much more at this stage, but if the mystery is solved, I'll be sure to let you know!"

As she got up to leave, Ayesha thanked Emina for her help and hospitality and exchanged contact details with her so that they could keep in touch. Ayesha had a feeling that she would be speaking to Emina again soon, if not for more information about Ibn Arabi, then at least to continue their new friendship.

While walking out of the Suleymaniye complex, Ayesha thought carefully about what Emina had told her. She thought it was very interesting that the fabled lost manuscript happened to be a copy of *The Seven Days of the Heart*. While she did not like jumping to conclusions, Ayesha thought that the information Emina had provided somehow fit the description implied in the hidden note. She remembered that the author of the note wrote about knowledge of the *Shaykh al-Akbar*, and the message said that "The Seven are not lost." Ayesha felt sure that "The Seven" referred to in the hidden note must mean Ibn Arabi's missing manuscript!

Ayesha was happy that Emina had provided her with a solid lead for the mysterious note. She could not wait to discuss the day's events with her friends.

***

Ayesha found Sara and Jess at the café opposite the Suleymaniye complex where they had earlier agreed to meet for lunch. The small café had only a couple of tables and there was not much on the menu except *pide*. This suited them, as they just wanted a quick lunch.

The girls caught up on the last few hours while they sat at a small round table eating hot, fresh spinach and feta cheese *pide* in paper lunch bags. Ayesha told the others about what she had found out about the *Awrad-al-Usbu* by Ibn Arabi being *The Seven Days of the Heart*. She also recounted how the librarian called Berke had crept up on her in the library archives.

"What a weirdo!" exclaimed Sara. "That's just creepy. Do you think he might have some information about the missing manuscript?"

"Or perhaps he wants to look for it himself, and wants to find out what you know about it?" Jess suggested.

Ayesha added, "I don't know, but it seems that we may not be the only ones interested in 'The Seven'!"

Ayesha reached into her bag and pulled out the small blue purse where she was keeping the hidden note. She took out the note and studied it again before saying, "I guess the next step is to follow the clues given in this note."

Ayesha read out Emre's English translation of the note:

"The Seven are not lost.

They are hidden for their own protection.

They belong together in the Suleymaniye Kutuphanesi but the time is not right.

I pray that you are true, and that your heart is clear.

What you seek contains the knowledge of the Shaykh al-Akbar.

Within the forbidden place.

Become one with the mirror.

Look beyond it to find your heart's desire."

Sara looked up from her delicious *pide* and addressed Jess. "Jessie, what was it that the museum guide was saying about the harem in the palace, and about it being forbidden or something?"

Jess perked up, "Oh yeah! The guide at the museum was telling us a bit about the Topkapi Palace. It was first built by the sultan in the 1400s after he conquered the city, and the palace became the residence of the sultans from that time. It was also the place from where the day-to-day running of the empire was carried out for 400 years."

Jess continued, "Anyway, within the palace was a huge harem section, where all the sultan's women were kept."

Sara interjected, "The women were slaves and they had been bought for the sultan from slave markets all over the Ottoman Empire. Of course, all of them had to be pretty enough for the Sultan!"

Ayesha grimaced in sympathy. "Oh, those poor women!" she cried.

Jess nodded and explained, "It was forbidden

for any males except the sultan, and the African eunuch slaves, to enter the harem."

"So do you think the harem could be 'the forbidden place' that is mentioned in the note?" Sara asked.

"Well, I guess it's probably the most famous 'forbidden place' in this country and also the whole former Ottoman Empire," Ayesha remarked. "Perhaps we should pay a visit to the harem and find out!"

***

Ayesha and the girls caught a tram to the Topkapi Palace, which was in the historic part of the city not too far away from their hotel. The closest tram stop was about a five-minute walk away from the entrance to the palace. The friends chatted amiably while they walked, admiring the city as they went.

All of the streets in this section of the old town

were bustling with traffic and crowds of people walking along the pavement. Ayesha could smell the faint scent of pollution from the traffic, which was overtaken every now and then by the delicious aroma of hot street food coming from the roadside food stalls that were set up along the numerous city garden paths in this area of town.

There were plenty of tourists out and about in the Sultanahmet area of Istanbul, but Ayesha mostly enjoyed observing the local women going about their everyday lives. She noticed that many of the older women wore traditionally patterned hijabs tied up in the local style, whereas there was a mixture of clothing styles among the young. Some chose a more traditional dress, while others dressed in the latest fashions. Whether or not the outfit included a hijab appeared to be personal preference.

The girls made their way towards a large city park with luscious colourful garden beds. The park was framed on one side by a busy street that housed various shopfronts on the other side of the street. On the far side of the park was a high stone wall, which marked the beginning of the palace grounds. As they were walking through the park, Ayesha heard her name being called out from behind her. She turned around to see Emre waving at her from the road. Ayesha smiled as he walked towards her. She'd forgotten how handsome he was.

Emre smiled as he reached her. "I thought it was you from the road but I was too far away to be sure. I took my chances and came this way. I'm glad I did!"

Ayesha laughed, "What are you doing here? I thought you were working today."

"I was in my father's shop this morning, and then he wanted me to drop a book to one of his good customers who lives nearby. So here I am,"

Emre said. "My father told me to take the rest of the day off. Are you on the way to the Topkapi Palace at the end of this park?"

"We sure are," Ayesha said.

"Why don't you come and be our guide?" Sara chipped in.

Ayesha felt her heart lift a little at the thought of being accompanied by Emre for their tour of the palace. Ayesha caught Sara giving Jess a wink and a small nudge.

"Here goes," Ayesha thought, "I'm going to be grilled by these two about Emre back at the hotel tonight." She smiled on the inside. He had been really helpful with the note, and he'd been kind to them the day before, even though they had only just met. Ayesha happily walked on, excited to be spending more time with Emre and her friends, and led the group towards the palace entrance.

Once they were inside the palace gates, Emre explained that the palace comprised four main courtyards and many smaller buildings within its complex. He informed the girls that the palace used to house thousands of people and contained mosques, bakeries, a hospital, and even a mint for making money.

Emre led the girls through the first courtyard, which was where dignitaries and people coming to visit the Sultan would wait while dressed in their best clothing. As the group of friends walked through the extensive courtyard, Ayesha reminded Emre about the note, saying that what they were seeking was within "the forbidden place." She told Emre that they were guessing that the forbidden place mentioned in the note might be the harem of the palace. Emre agreed that it was possible and they should investigate. As he was aware of the sheer size of the palace grounds, he tried to guide them through the palace courtyards at a quick pace.

The group had a cursory look around the

second courtyard that hosted the administrative buildings from which the Ottoman Empire was run. Emre pointed out the Tower of Justice, which represented the justice of the sultan, the palace kitchens, and the stables. The entrance to the harem was also located off this courtyard, but Emre told Ayesha that there was something else he wanted to show her first.

Emre led them into the third courtyard, which housed the sultan's chambers and the Hall of Audience where the sultan used to accept ambassadors and dignitaries. He caught Ayesha's eye as he excitedly beckoned her towards the Privy Chambers of the Sultan. "You'll want to see this Ayesha," Emre smiled as he stepped aside to let her in.

Ayesha walked into a room with its walls and ceiling decorated with colourful, enamelled tiles in different geometric designs. High above the walls Ayesha could see beautiful inscriptions of the

Quran highlighted in exquisite royal blue. The melodious voice of a skilled *muezzin* who was reading the Quran filled the air, and Ayesha looked around to see the *muezzin* himself sitting in a special glass-walled room, reading into a microphone.

Ayesha looked gratefully at Emre and nodded, "You were right, this place is awesome."

Emre smiled and said, "Hang on, we haven't seen the best thing yet."

The inside of the room was filled with glass displays of various items from around the palace. Emre led Ayesha around a few displays and stopped in front of a display showcasing a large ancient sword and archer's bow. He pointed at the display and asked her, "Whose do you think these are?"

Ayesha shook her head, "I don't know. Please tell me," she prompted.

Emre looked gravely towards the display and

gently put his hand on the glass. "This is the sword and bow of our Blessed Prophet Muhammad, peace be upon him. Can you imagine that he once held these things in his hands over 1400 years ago?"

Ayesha's heart seemed to swell as she looked with renewed interest at the sword and bow on display. It was overwhelming to imagine that these items had belonged to the Prophet, and that he had touched them and used them during his lifetime. Ayesha felt that by just seeing and being close to the Prophet's worldly belongings, it somehow made her feel as if the Prophet were near. It gave her a stronger sense of feeling his presence in this world as a man and a real human being.

Emre led Ayesha around to several other displays containing other treasured relics of the Islamic world, and her eyes were filled with tears by the time they had finished exploring the section. They had lost the others some time ago, so they waited at the building's exit for Sara and Jess to make their way through.

While they were waiting, Ayesha thanked Emre again for taking her through the Privy Chambers of the Sultan. She had had no idea that items of the Blessed Prophet were kept in the Topkapi Palace. She would remember this moment for the rest of her life.

Emre smiled at her. "I'm so glad I was lucky enough to be the one to show you. It's amazing isn't it? It's a good reminder that we will also one day be gone from this life."

Ayesha nodded and smiled back at him. "And a good reminder to be aware of life's bigger picture, because everything we see is temporary."

Ayesha looked up to see Jess and Sara meandering through the exit towards them. She noticed a twinkle in Sara's eye. "Ah! It seems that Sara lost me *juuust* a little bit on purpose!" Ayesha thought. "I'll have to follow that up with her later!"

The group walked back to the entrance of the harem in the second courtyard. It was now about three o'clock in the afternoon and the palace would be closing in a couple of hours. Luckily, there was not much of a queue to enter the harem section. Emre told the others that the line of visitors to get into the harem could often be quite long, especially when the weather was nice.

Today, Ayesha and her friends thankfully only had to wait for a few tourists who were in the queue before them. They had just stepped into a long dimly lit hallway leading into the section when they heard a loud scream from deeper within the harem!

CHAPTER SIX

Ayesha ran towards the direction of the scream from within the harem. She could hear Emre running behind her. Ayesha ran down the long corridor until she came to a flight of steep descending steps. At the bottom of the steps, there was an elderly Turkish woman sitting down and clutching her ankle. The woman was weeping in pain. Ayesha ran down the stairs to help her. "Oh dear! Are you alright?" she asked.

The woman looked up at Ayesha gratefully and pointed to the last step. "I fell. Last step…" the woman grimaced in pain while holding onto her ankle. Emre arrived at the scene and Ayesha asked him to go and get some help while she stayed with the woman. Ayesha crouched down and checked the woman's legs for any obvious broken bones. All the pain seemed to be centred in the woman's ankle.

Ayesha knew it wasn't a good idea to move the ankle. She tried to calm the woman down as much as possible, speaking soothing words and giving her some water from the bottle inside her bag.

The woman held onto Ayesha's hands and pointed towards another corridor. "My English no good. My husband go toilet. So much pain…"

Ayesha felt sorry for the woman and stayed with her until her husband came back. When he saw his wife on the ground, his face dropped and he ran to see if she was alright.

In a few moments, Emre came back with the paramedics who examined the injured woman's ankle and gave her some tablets to relieve the pain. Thankfully, other than the ankle and the shock of falling, there was no further injury. As the woman lay on a stretcher, about to be taken to the hospital, she gestured towards Ayesha and took her hand. "You are very kind. I would like to thank you. What is your name? I am Rabia Aga."

"I'm Ayesha Dean," Ayesha smiled kindly. "Please take care of yourself and I hope you get better soon."

The woman's husband gave Ayesha a grateful smile. "Thank you for looking after my wife. I feel bad I was not there when she fell."

"It wasn't your fault, Uncle," she respectfully addressed the older man. "*Alhamdulillah* it was not more serious."

Ayesha and her friends waited until the paramedics had left before continuing their hunt for more clues regarding the mysterious note. The group walked through several dimly lit corridors before reaching another section of rooms in the harem. The map told them that this sparsely furnished area was where the eunuchs would guard the harem day and night.

The plain, bare walls of this section fit the picture in Ayesha's mind of what an ancient guardroom would have looked like. She had heard that in the time of the sultans, anyone who was not authorised couldn't get in or out of the harem unless they got past the guards who were stationed here.

The group walked further and further into the harem and saw endless rooms and hallways. It felt as if they could get easily lost inside this place, so they kept referring back to the map whenever they entered a new section. Emre announced that he was not familiar with the harem section as he usually didn't have enough time or inclination to queue up and explore this area of the palace.

Ayesha observed that some of the rooms were grand and beautiful, with detailed wall mosaics and colourful enamelled tiling. The mosque area had beautiful Quranic scripture decorating its colourful walls, and Ayesha imagined that the many fountains and empty pools littering the harem would have once been a beautiful sight when they were in operation.

Although the harem was beautiful, there appeared to be no means of escape to the outside world. Ayesha realised that the inhabitants of the harem could have caught filtered sunlight through the intricately latticed walls and ceilings, but they wouldn't have had any unobstructed view to the world beyond the harem. Ayesha felt sad, knowing that all those people living in the harem must have felt like prisoners inside these beautiful walls.

After over an hour of exploring, Sara's stomach made a loud rumbling noise. She laughed and put her hand to her stomach. "Guys, I think that's a sign that I'm hungry and we should get moving!"

Jess agreed wholeheartedly, "It's been so lovely exploring this gorgeous palace, but I'm also getting hungry. What are we looking for again?"

Ayesha laughed and said, "*Within the forbidden place. Become one with the mirror. Look beyond it to find your heart's desire.*" Ayesha looked at Emre, "You don't happen to know of any mirrors in this section do you?"

Emre replied, "Well there's the large mirror I saw near the guardroom area. That's the only one I can think of, although there might be others around, I'm not sure."

"Let's go back there then," Ayesha said.

When they got back near the guardroom area, they saw a very large mirror hanging in a recess within the large room. The mirror was framed in gold with a very intricately decorated and solid-looking frame.

"How on earth did we miss this before?" Sara exclaimed.

Ayesha laughed, "Yeah I don't know, it's huge!"

Ayesha went to stand directly in front of the imposing mirror. *"Become one with the mirror,"* she murmured as she gazed into its reflection. Ayesha could see that there was another smaller mirror behind her, giving the illusion that there was an infinite number of mirrors before her and behind her. Ayesha repeated to herself, *"Look beyond it to find your heart's desire."*

All Ayesha could see when she looked into the mirror, was herself, and then beyond that, the reflection of the mirror behind her, causing an impression that there were multiple Ayeshas. "Is this some sort of metaphor?" Ayesha wondered. "Is the journey to myself or within myself my heart's desire? Hmmm, Ibn Arabi is already having an impact on my thinking," she happily pondered. Ayesha racked her brains trying to think of what the note could mean. She remembered that Ibn Arabi often wrote of the importance of seeing the true reality of things.

Noticing a small, darker spot on the white wall in the reflection of the mirror, Ayesha turned around and walked to the wall behind her. Just under the opposite mirror on the wall was a small etching. She called the others over, "Look! Something is carved into the wall. Can you see what it says?"

They all bent over to look at the wall more closely. Emre said, "It looks like a four and a zero. Forty?"

Jess exclaimed, "Wait, there's something next to it. It looks like a shape, a zigzag shape."

Sara jumped in, "The number forty, and a zigzag going down. Is this what we were looking for? What could it mean?"

"The *Forty Steps*!" Ayesha said excitedly to the others.

Emre smiled, "Yes! You could be right."

Sara and Jess looked expectantly at Ayesha. Ayesha explained, "The Forty Steps make up the famous stairway that led to the harem's hospital. It can be accessed by the Courtyard of the Concubines and Favourite Wives of the Sultan. I read about this in a history magazine when we were planning the trip, how lucky!"

"I think we actually passed that courtyard earlier," said Emre. "We just need to retrace our steps."

Using their map for guidance, the group found their way to the Courtyard of the Concubines and Chief Consorts. It was a relatively small courtyard compared to the harem's numerous other courtyards. Behind tall porticoes, the courtyard was surrounded by the baths of the concubines, known as the *hamam*, the laundry fountain, the kitchen, dormitories and apartments of the former chief wives of the Sultan. The group of friends saw that the entrance to the apartment of the former Queen Mother was decorated with paintwork depicting scenic landscapes in the Western European style.

The group moved on towards the right hand side of the courtyard where they found a room referred to in their map as the "Long Room". The information pamphlet told them that in the past, this room was usually heated with a large stove. An archway next to the long room marked the beginning of the Forty Steps, the stairway that led to the harem hospital.

"OK, so here we are," Ayesha announced. "We may as well check it out and see if we can find something!"

"What are we looking for, though?" Jess asked.

"I'm not exactly sure," Ayesha responded. "But perhaps look for any loose pieces of stone in the stairs. That would be a good start."

"Perhaps we should each take a section of the stairs to look at," Sara suggested.

"Great idea," agreed Ayesha. "I'll go down and take the bottom ten."

"I'll take the ten above Ayesha's," called out Sara.

"I'll take the ten above Sara's," said Jess.

"That leaves me with the top ten then," said Emre as they all moved towards the archway leading down the stairs.

Ayesha counted the steps as she walked down until she reached the bottom ten steps. Luckily, there was no one else besides the four friends in the stairway, so they didn't have to contend with other tourists walking around and wondering what they were doing.

On the tenth step from the bottom, Ayesha walked slowly along the length of the step to see whether there were any loose pieces of stone. There did not appear to be any looseness in the step at all. It was solid, and none of the stone was moving anywhere.

Ayesha repeated the process of walking very slowly along the length of each of her allocated ten steps, one by one, to see if she could find any loose parts within the stairs. After getting to the bottom step and not finding anything, she called out to the others, "Anyone having any luck?"

"Not me," called out Sara.

"Nothing here," called Emre.

"Same here," called Jess.

"Hmm," mused Ayesha as she leant heavily against the wall. Her bag caught awkwardly between her back and the wall, resulting in something rather hard poking into her back. Ayesha grimaced in unexpected discomfort and thought it was probably the sunglasses case in her bag that had caused the problem. She stood up straight again and rubbed her back where her bag had poked into her.

Just then, Ayesha heard a soft sound like the crumbling of stone. She looked down at her feet and noticed what appeared to be tiny pieces of stone and dust that she hadn't noticed earlier. "That's funny," she thought. "I wonder if I've stumbled onto something."

Ayesha turned around and examined the wall she had just been leaning on. The wall was built of stone. Ayesha bent down to take a closer look. Using her hands, she followed the trail of stone dust upwards to about knee height, where the trail of dust seemed to stop. She gently started knocking on the stone brick that seemed to have released the loose stone. She thought that perhaps some of the loose stone may have been released when she had slumped against the wall. When the others saw Ayesha working at the piece of stone in the wall, they came down to see what was happening.

"Ayesha, be careful," warned Jess worriedly. "There are security guards around and they may think you're damaging the building."

"I'll be careful," Ayesha said quietly. "I don't think any damage will be done. Look here, this stone is already loose!"

Ayesha gently manoeuvred a small piece of stone away from the wall. The stone had been jammed into place, but now that Ayesha had removed it, she could see that there was a very small hole in the wall, smaller than the size of her fist. She saw that something small had been placed within the hole. She gently put her hand inside to see what it was.

Picking up the object, Ayesha felt a thrill of excitement move through her body. She held the item up for the others to see.

In her hand, Ayesha held a small key!

CHAPTER SEVEN

Ayesha put the key inside her purse for safe-keeping and motioned for her friends to help her place the stone back into the wall. Once the stone was firmly back in place, the friends hurriedly ascended the Forty Steps and made their way out of the harem. A short time later, they casually walked out of the grounds of the Topkapi Palace into the adjacent city parklands.

"I don't know about you guys," announced Sara, "but I'm starving."

The others laughed and expressed their

agreement. Ayesha found that she had also built up an appetite after all the tension of searching for clues within the palace.

"My car is not far from here," Emre mentioned. "Why don't I give you all a lift to your hotel? We can stop in to see my father on the way there. He said he would write down the name of the person who supplied the book of maps."

"That's a great idea!" agreed Ayesha.

After a short car ride to the markets, Ayesha and her friends walked into Mehmet's shop. Mehmet was overjoyed to see Ayesha and the girls together with his son.

"*Merhaba,* Ayesha, my lovely customer!" he exclaimed, while wiping the dust from a book he was holding between his hands. "I am very happy to see you and your friends again."

Ayesha smiled and greeted the older man fondly. "Very happy to see you again too," she said. Ayesha couldn't resist taking a quick gaze around the familiar shop before continuing. "We are sorry to bother you, but Emre was saying that you could tell us the name of the person who sold you that beautiful book of maps that I bought the other day?"

Mehmet placed the book he was holding in a nearby cabinet, and turned to her. "Yes of course. Emre said that you found a note hidden inside the book. This is very interesting for me. I told this wonderful story to some of my customers today!" he beamed. "I use it as…aah, how do you say? An advertisement for my shop!"

Ayesha continued smiling at the well-meaning bookseller and brushed aside the small sense of disquiet that Mehmet's words brought to her. He obviously didn't think there was any harm in telling everyone about the note. Hopefully, the people he had told were not of the unscrupulous sort that Uncle Dave had warned her against.

Ayesha asked, "Have you told many people about the note?"

Mehmet responded, "Only my long-time customers, a husband and wife who have come to my bookshop for years. They are very good customers." He stared thoughtfully into the distance and began to think of new ways to advertise his shop now that a hidden note had been discovered.

After a moment, Ayesha said, "Thank you for letting us know who supplied the book to you. That would be really helpful for us in trying to solve the puzzle."

Mehmet was brought back from his reverie. "Ah yes, the person who sold me the box of books," he muttered to himself. "Now where did I put that paper?"

"Oh, Dad!" Emre groaned good-naturedly. "You didn't leave it in the food pantry like you left the keys last week did you?"

Mehmet laughed. "No, my son. It is here, in my pocket." He handed the piece of paper to Ayesha. Ayesha saw that Mehmet had handwritten a name and an address.

Mehmet added, "I am sorry the man did not leave me his phone number. But he gave me his address. He insisted that I buy more items from him in future."

Ayesha thanked Mehmet for his information and resolved to pay the supplier a visit the next day. Right now, Ayesha knew that there was a delicious Turkish dinner awaiting them at the hotel. *Alhamdulillah*, Emre could drop them straight there!

***

The next morning Ayesha, Sara and Jess went to the hotel lobby to ask Mrs Nurhan for help with directions. They were hoping to pay a visit to the supplier, a man named Arslan Avci.

"Ah, let's see," said Mrs Nurhan from behind

the lobby desk as she took the paper out of Ayesha's hand and pushed her glasses further up her nose. Mrs Nurhan reminded Ayesha of the quintessential hotel matron. She had flouncy, dyed brown hair, and smelled strongly of Chanel No. 5 perfume. The matron was wearing a printed floral blouse done up tightly to her neck, where she had pinned a gold, oval-shaped, cameo brooch.

Mrs Nurhan pointed at the map, which was spread out over the counter. "You will need to catch the tram to this area near the Grand Bazaar, then turn down this street…wait, let me mark it for you on the map."

The girls waited while Mrs Nurhan helpfully marked the best route for the girls to take. Ayesha didn't know if the address they had been given was a business or a residential house. She hoped that someone would be there to see them when they got there.

After the tram ride to a different part of town,

Ayesha and her two friends stepped off the small platform and crossed the street. They turned down the street that Mrs Nurhan had marked on the map. The street was not a main street and there was no traffic on the road. It was lined with old terrace houses that had seen better days, and there were some two-storey buildings that looked like they were in a similar, worn-out state. A few old locals were strolling on the footpaths, but there was nobody else around. The paint on most of the buildings was peeling away, but it appeared to Ayesha that the buildings looked solid, and could probably last another hundred years.

The girls walked almost to the end of the dead-end street before turning right into another smaller street. This street was so narrow that it could have been better described as a laneway. It was wide enough to let motorbikes through, and possibly very small cars if they were travelling in only one direction. The laneway was lined with old, two-storey buildings, which were in an even greater state of disrepair than the buildings that the girls had passed earlier. Ayesha could detect the faint whiff of sewerage and garbage in the air, and she tried to put it out of her mind.

The three friends studied the buildings' numbers as they passed each one. Some of the numbers had been worn away from the front of the buildings. When they reached their destination, they looked up to see a narrow, two-storey house with a simple façade. The building had once been white, but had aged through neglect and had become a greyish colour. There was one single window upstairs, as well as a single grimy window downstairs. On the door there was a sign in Turkish that the girls could not understand, but it appeared to Ayesha to signify that this building may have housed some sort of business. Just next to the building was a small space where a bicycle that was connected to a large cart for carrying goods was parked.

"Here goes," Ayesha said as she knocked on the door. "I hope someone is around."

To Ayesha's surprise, the door swung inward as soon as she knocked. There was nobody on the other side. Ayesha tentatively pushed the door open a bit further. The sound of loud heavy metal music filled the air and seemed to be coming from upstairs.

"Hello! Is anybody there?" Ayesha called out. Nobody answered, so she called out again. "Helloooo!..." There was still no answer.

Ayesha looked at Sara and Jess with round eyes. "What do you think? Shall we go upstairs, it sounds like someone's around…"

Jess appeared hesitant and looked around her. "I don't know…We don't seem to be in the safest of areas."

"I know!" Sara interjected. "How about two of us go up, and one stay out here just in case. Then at least one of us can call for help if anything dodgy happens."

"Jess could stay out here as our back up," agreed Ayesha. "Always better to be safe than sorry." Jess agreed, and Ayesha and Sara stepped into the building.

Ayesha and Sara walked slowly up the narrow, creaky, wooden stairs. It didn't appear that anyone was in the small area downstairs, and the girls could see that the downstairs room was filled with what appeared to be second-hand junk and various items in cardboard boxes. There was a strong smell of dampness and mould in the air.

Ayesha and Sara reached the small landing at the top of the stairs. They found themselves in front of a single closed door from which the sound of the metal music was blaring. Just as Ayesha was about to call out her presence, the girls heard the sound of an American male voice shouting in anger from inside the room, "I told him no! It has to be there by the end of day or else!"

Ayesha was faced with a moment of indecision. She thought, "Is there enough time for us to run back down before he notices us?"

Just then, the closed door swung open and a huge, angry-looking man in a sweaty, blue singlet-top stood in front of them. His arms were heavily tattooed, he wore a manicured moustache and goatee, and his head was shaved.

"Umm, hello!" said Ayesha quickly. "We were looking for Arslan and were given this address. Do you know where we may find him?"

The man replied in a gruff voice, "Who are you? And do you always enter without knocking?"

"My name's Ayesha Dean, and I'm sorry to have just showed up like this, but I don't think you heard us when we knocked downstairs."

The man stalked back into the room and turned down the music. Ayesha could see that this room was also filled with knick-knacks and items that were all over the floor, as well as covering the shelves of the walls. The man returned from switching down the music. "I am Arslan. What do you want?"

Ayesha noticed that he spoke with an American accent and thought that he must have spent a significant amount of time overseas to have picked it up. Ayesha spoke up, "We were given your name by Mehmet from the Old Book Bazaar. I bought a beautiful book from him the other day and I loved it so much I wondered where it came from."

"What book was it?" Arslan asked.

"It was an old book of maps and it was in a box of other old books, all in very good condition," Ayesha replied.

"Do you have the book with you?" Arslan asked. "I deliver a lot of items. You can't expect me to remember each one."

The three of them were still standing on the small landing upstairs. The man had not invited the girls to take a seat anywhere. "Just as well," Ayesha thought. "It would be a struggle to find any place to sit among all the clutter."

Thankfully Ayesha had brought the book of maps with her today. She pulled it out of her tote bag and passed it to Arslan. He took it from her and started looking through it quickly.

"What's so special about this book?" growled Arslan. He looked at Ayesha more closely. "Is there something about it you're not telling me?"

Ayesha played dumb and acted like a besotted tourist. "I just love all these old books and since we're in Istanbul I thought it would be interesting to trace the history of my first book purchase in this city, that's all."

Arslan looked as if he didn't believe her and

continued studying the book. Ayesha thought, "Thank God, Sara stitched up the hole in the back, even though it was not the greatest fix-up job. Hopefully he won't look too closely."

Ayesha's heart sank as she saw Arslan notice a defect in the back of the book cover. There was still a bit of a bulge in the cover where the hidden note had been placed. Fortunately, Ayesha knew the note was safely inside her purse. Last night she had placed the small key that they had found inside the Topkapi Palace into the little safe inside her hotel room. At least she knew that the key was safely back at the hotel.

Ayesha noticed that Arslan had suddenly become still and thoughtful. "What do we have here?" Arslan asked as he examined the bulge in the back of the book cover. He then looked more closely at Sara's irregular stitching of the leather seams, before quickly looking up at Ayesha in an intimidating manner. "There was something inside here wasn't there?" he demanded.

"Oh yeah it was nothing," Ayesha said dismissively. "Just some little note in Turkish. I couldn't understand it."

Arslan smirked, "So that's how you're playing it eh? Huh, well it's nothing to me anyway. Why come all this way to find me if it was nothing?"

Ayesha just shrugged her shoulders, pretending that she didn't really care. "Just a bit of fun, and an excuse to find out more about this city and its people," she responded.

"Alright then Ayesha Dean," Arslan said, still suspicious. "I can tell you where I got this book from. As I said, it's nothing to me. Unless you're going to be stealing my business?" He gruffly piped up again.

"No, of course not," Ayesha responded. "I'm only visiting here in Sultanahmet for a short while."

"Are you staying in the Hagia Sophia tourist

region?" he asked.

"Well, yeah, we are real tourists. I can assure you I'm not planning on stealing any of your business," Ayesha responded calmly.

Arslan relaxed his shoulders, which had been bunched up with tension. "OK, I can only tell you the address it came from. My source was very secretive and he didn't want me to know his name. I didn't ask any questions because he wanted to get rid of what he called, "His Uncle's junk," and I got the whole box for a fairly decent price. I made a bit of a profit when I sold the books to Mehmet."

Arslan continued, "I picked up the box from my source at his house in the Beyoglu area."

He told the girls the address and Sara quickly typed it into her phone, which she had in her hand. Ayesha asked, "So how did you get in touch with your source if you didn't know his name?"

"This is how I make my living," Arslan responded. "Buying off people who want to get rid of their junk, and selling it to other shops or whoever wants to buy it. Been doing it for years after coming back from the USA. An acquaintance of mine told me this guy had some decent stuff to sell so I turned up at the address and told the guy I could move it that day. I guess he wanted the money quickly and I was conveniently there. Strange guy. Living in that posh house and selling all that stuff like he was desperate and stressed. Huh, he could come live in this place instead and see how he feels then."

Arslan then gruffly asked Ayesha if that was all, as he wanted to be left in peace. Ayesha and Sara thanked him for his time and made their way back downstairs. Arslan immediately went inside his room and turned the heavy metal music back onto full blast.

As the three friends gathered outside the house, Ayesha saw a shadow of a person watching them from the upstairs window. "It must be Arslan," Ayesha thought. "He was an odd character, but quite helpful."

Ayesha felt a little anxious that another person now knew about the hidden note, but Arslan had said that the note meant nothing to him. Ayesha hoped that telling Arslan about the note would not threaten their investigation in any way!

CHAPTER EIGHT

After their encounter with Arslan, Ayesha, Sara, and Jess made their way back to the nearest tram stop. A helpful lady who was passing by gave them information on how to get to the Beyoglu area of Istanbul, which was where the address of Arslan's unnamed 'source' was located. The three friends followed the lady's directions and walked over the Galata Bridge, which connected the Sultanahmet area to Beyoglu over the Golden Horn. The Golden Horn was the flooded river valley connecting the Bosphorus and the Sea of

Marmara. From there, they took the Tünel up the hill, enjoying the ride on the second-oldest subway in the world. The friends then found themselves walking along the well-known Istiklal Avenue, one of the main streets in Beyoglu. The avenue was filled with local people who were out and about enjoying the sunshine and sitting at the many trendy cafes and restaurants lining the thoroughfare. There was a lively buzz in the air as plenty of university students and young professionals got together with friends to chat and enjoy the festive atmosphere on this side of town.

Sara suggested that they should stop somewhere for lunch, so the girls found a tiny hole-in-the-wall eatery selling tasty Turkish wraps, or *durum* as the locals called it. Sitting on stools at the skinny bar on one side of the shop, the three friends enjoyed delicious grilled chicken kebabs wrapped in freshly made, pizza-type bread, along with freshly chopped parsley, spices, onion and tomatoes.

"Yum, this is soooo delicious!" Sara exclaimed while tucking into another bite of her *durum* wrap.

"This is probably the best kebab I've ever tasted!" agreed Jess. "This bread is amazing!"

Ayesha laughed, "As always, one of the best things about travelling is the food! There's no way you can go past delicious *durum*, breads and pastries when you're in Istanbul!"

As Jess tilted her head to take another bite of her *durum*, a large chunk of kebab fell out of her wrap and rolled onto the bar table. "Oh no!" she exclaimed in dismay as she eyed the succulent piece of food on the table.

"Ten-second rule!" Sara exclaimed as she picked up Jess's fallen kebab and popped it into her own mouth.

"No Sara! You don't know if this table's been wiped! And that ten-second-rule thing is not a true rule anyway," warned Jess.

"I'll be 'right!" Sara shrugged. "Why waste a perfectly good piece of chicken kebab?"

Ayesha grinned, "It's a win-win situation all 'round!"

They finished off their lunch with a refreshing *ayran* yoghurt drink and continued on their way. Ayesha loved looking at the many grand old buildings in this area that were situated alongside more modern architecture. The friends spent some time enjoying the lively atmosphere by taking a short ride on a historic red tram along Istiklal Avenue, and then listening to the live music coming out of various establishments along La Rue Francaise.

They grabbed a coffee at a gorgeous outside café near Taksim Square, where they observed the interesting Monument of the Republic, which commemorated the formation of the Turkish Republic.

At Taksim Square, the friends stopped and used their map to find the address that Arslan had given them. Ayesha noticed that their intended destination was only a few streets away from the square. There appeared to be a lot of important buildings on the main streets of this area. The address of Arslan's source was located on a small side street that had a number of residences.

The friends found their way to the correct street and walked up to the address they were looking for. There was a large, peach-coloured stone wall separating the building from the pavement. Beyond the wall, the girls could see a rather imposing two-storey residence, built in an eighteenth-century European style.

Ayesha noticed that the only means of entry to the residence was through the secure electronic gate. There was an intercom next to the gate and Ayesha pressed the button to speak to the occupants. There was no answer.

After about five minutes of trying the buzzer with no response, the girls began to discuss whether they should leave and come back in a few hours. Suddenly, a woman's voice called out from behind them, "Ayesha! Ayesha!"

The friends turned around and saw an elderly woman in a wheelchair being pushed by an elderly man. Ayesha recognised the woman as being the same woman who had fallen down the stairs at the Topkapi Palace the other day. She quickly scanned her memory and remembered that the woman's name was Rabia Aga.

Rabia was smiling and waving at her, and she beckoned Ayesha and her friends to come over to them across the quiet street. "*Merhaba*, Ayesha! I am so happy to see you again." Rabia pointed to a small and pretty house nearby and said in halting English, "This is my home. What a good day for visit! Please come in for tea, I am so happy for you and your friends to visit me."

***

A short time later, Ayesha and her friends were seated at a round table inside Rabia's cosy kitchen, enjoying the delicious smell of freshly baked Turkish shortbread cookies. Rabia was sitting in her wheelchair, which was pushed up to the table, while her husband Ozhan was pottering around the kitchen making tea for the guests. In the middle of the table sat a large silver serving dish filled with homemade Turkish cookies.

"We just made them," Rabia said, indicating the cookies. "Please help yourself."

Ozhan finished serving the tea in small Turkish tea glasses then sat down at the table. He addressed Ayesha, "I am so thankful for your kindness to my wife the other day. We are getting older, and it is harder to do many things. Just walking is difficult now. It can be very hard for us."

"I'm just sorry that Rabia had that fall. But I'm glad I was there to help," said Ayesha as she took a bite of a delicious cookie. "Oh these cookies are incredible!" she exclaimed. After a few moments Ayesha continued, "May I ask you something about your neighbour across the road? The one in the big house with the pink wall?"

"Oh, that house, yes," replied Ozhan. "My neighbour lived there for a long time. He passed away one month ago."

"Did you know him well?" asked Ayesha.

"Not very well. We have been here only about one year. Before he died, my neighbour Aksoy told me that he lived there a long time. He was a nice neighbour but very sick all the time."

"Aksoy," Sara repeated. "Was that his name?"

"Yes, Mr Aksoy. He was a nice man. But we are from a different world to him. We were not close friends. *Alhamdulillah*, now we live in this beautiful house. But only because our son helped us. We were always poor. I did not know what to say to Mr Aksoy who was very rich."

Ayesha smiled, "You and your wife are such a kind-hearted couple, I'm sure anyone would be honoured to be your friends."

There was a short pause in the conversation while everyone slowly sipped their hot tea. Jess then spoke up, "How old was Mr Aksoy when he passed away?"

Ozhan looked at his wife quizzically as Rabia shrugged her shoulders. He responded, "I am not sure but maybe about 80 years old. Lately we see a younger man coming in and out of the house, but we have not met him. He always looks very busy. Coming in and out."

"Do you think he lives there, or perhaps he is just visiting?" Ayesha asked.

"I don't know," replied Ozhan. "He comes and goes at different times of the day. I am sorry, I do not know much about him."

"That's alright," replied Ayesha. "He may have some information that we're looking for that's all."

Rabia and Ozhan could provide no more information about their neighbour, and the conversation naturally moved on to whether the girls had been enjoying their stay in Istanbul, and all the sites they had seen. The girls found that the elderly couple were extremely hospitable and welcoming. They thoroughly enjoyed spending time with the local couple and sharing their delicious homemade cookies.

**

About an hour later, the girls said goodbye and thank you to Ozhan and Rabia. Rabia gave Ayesha a big hug and placed a small plastic container full of cookies into her hands. "These are for later," she smiled.

Ayesha and her friends then made their way across the road, back to the big house with the pink stone wall. Ayesha pressed the intercom button and waited. After several minutes there was still no answer. They decided it would best to leave. They had a lot to discuss and they still had to make their way back to the Sultanahmet area before it got dark. As they turned away to head back to their hotel, they didn't notice the slight movement of a curtain dropping back into place in the upstairs window of the house.

***

Later that evening, Ayesha and her friends caught up with Uncle Dave and Sara's father for dinner at a lovely restaurant not far from the hotel. Ayesha was looking forward to catching up with Uncle Dave, as the men had been very busy with work and she hadn't had a chance to update him about their recent findings.

The intimate restaurant was sumptuously decorated in maroon and gold wall fabric, with traditional maroon and gold coloured tassels attached at each corner and angle of the walls. Ayesha and her group were seated in a private alcove adjacent to the main seating area. Their table was laden with various bowls and dishes filled with fluffy white rice, hot, tasty meat and vegetable stews, doner kebab, and plenty of fresh salads seasoned with mint and olive oil.

As they started their meal, Uncle Dave asked, "So how's the investigation about the mysterious note coming along?"

Sara spoke up as she helped herself to a generous serving of meat pilaf, "This is the perfect time for Ayesha to fill you in Uncle Dave, because right now this food is calling me…"

Everyone laughed. Ayesha responded, "Well, the most important thing I need to tell you is that we followed the clues in the note to find a key. It was hidden in the Topkapi Palace."

Uncle Dave raised his eyebrows, "A key?

Interesting…do you know what kind of key it is?"

"I'm not sure but it looks quite modern, and it is really small." Ayesha continued, "It's not as big as a house key or car key. I have a feeling it's a key to some sort of safe or something like that. I could show you when we get back to the hotel. I left it in the room safe."

"Hmmm, if it's a small key it could be a key to a safety deposit box," Uncle Dave mused. He took a sip of the freshly squeezed apple juice that they had each been served. "Oh wow, that's delicious!" He continued, "The problem is that there are plenty of banks with hundreds of safety deposit boxes all over this city. You would need more information to know where to look for it."

"We have a couple of clues, although I don't know what to make of them yet," said Ayesha. "The note told us that '*The Seven are not lost*', and what we are seeking contains '*the knowledge of the*

Shaykh al-Akbar', who you told us referred to Ibn Arabi. We found out that Ibn Arabi wrote some famous prayers called the *Awrad al-Usbu*, or *The Seven Days of the Heart.*"

Ayesha continued, "Apparently a beautiful manuscript of the *Awrad al-Usbu* was copied by one of Ibn Arabi's close disciples and has been missing for a hundred years. I have a feeling that the note could be referring to that missing manuscript!"

Uncle Dave let out a long whistle, "Sounds like you could be onto something. If the note is leading you to that manuscript, then you will really need to be careful. Whoever wrote the note was desperate enough to hide it from someone. Someone who, we might assume, was after the manuscript and probably up to no good."

Mr Isa, who up to this point had been concentrating on his meal as much as his daughter, then asked, "Have you looked into the name of whoever signed the note? It was signed wasn't it?"

Jess was keen to join the conversation and nodded, "The note was signed 'B.Ev'. Apparently Ev is not a common Turkish name. But we are going to look further into it. Emre told us it means 'home' or 'house'."

"Also," Ayesha added, "We found out that the book of maps came from a house belonging to a man called Mr Aksoy, who died about a month ago."

"Aksoy?" Mr Isa asked as he looked at Uncle Dave in a quizzical manner. "Isn't Aksoy the name of that building company that is quite famous around Turkey?"

Uncle Dave nodded, "Yeah, Aksoy, that's right. One of the Aksoy employees was attending our conference, and come to think of it, he did mention that the company figurehead had recently passed away."

Ayesha started drumming her fingers on the

table as her mind raced ahead. She felt Sara kick her feet under the table. "Ayesh!" whispered Sara. "Can you please stop that you're making me nervous."

"Sorry," Ayesha apologised. "I was just thinking...Do you think that *Ev*, or 'house', could be a metaphor for the author's building company?"

The occupants of the table all looked expectantly at Ayesha as she said, "Maybe the note was written by Mr Aksoy, signing as 'B.Ev' before he passed away!"

CHAPTER NINE

After a refreshing Turkish breakfast at the hotel the next morning, Ayesha arranged to meet Sara and Jess at the café across from the Hagia Sophia at around lunchtime. Each of the friends volunteered to do a bit of their own sleuthing this morning. Ayesha was going to catch a taxi to the offices of AKSOY to try and see whether she could find out any more clues about Mr Aksoy. Jess was going to search the telephone books for any people with the last name of Ev. Sara planned on finding out whether the little hidden key matched any particular safety deposit boxes within the city. Sara had taken several photos of the key with her phone and then placed the key back into the room safe as she didn't want it to get lost.

After Ayesha said goodbye to her friends, it took about half an hour for the taxi to drive her from the hotel into the business district of Istanbul. The taxi dropped Ayesha in front of a tall, glass building with a large sign on its door saying "AKSOY Ltd. Sti." The previous night Ayesha had run an internet search on the Chief Executive Officer of AKSOY Ltd. She had found out that his name was Mr Demir and Ayesha was hoping to be able to speak with him today.

Ayesha was wearing the most professional-looking outfit that she had brought on the trip. Luckily, she had thought to pack a black suit jacket that she could wear with her slim-line black pants and peach-coloured heels. She was wearing a white chiffon top underneath the jacket, and had tied her emerald green hijab behind her neck, styled in the shape of a bun behind her head. A chunky silver necklace and tasteful, silver drop earrings completed her look.

Ayesha walked into the enormous grey marble foyer and looked up at the ceiling, which was almost three stories high. It was an impressive space and she took a calming breath as she walked across to the reception desk on the opposite side of the foyer.

The desk was attended by three, sleek-looking, attractive women. It was difficult for Ayesha to tell them apart as they all wore the same fitted, charcoal-grey suits with a soft, tangerine-coloured top underneath. Their hair and make-up looked immaculate.

Ayesha went up to the woman whom she thought looked the friendliest of the three, even though none of them looked particularly friendly. "Hello, my name is Ayesha Dean. May I please see Mr Demir? I have something important that I wish to discuss with him."

"Do you have an appointment?" the woman asked.

Ayesha replied, "I don't but…"

"Well, I'm sorry, you cannot see Mr Demir without an appointment," the woman at the desk interrupted rudely.

"You don't understand. My father's…"

One of the other ladies at the desk who had overheard their conversation cut in, "Mr Demir is an extremely busy man. You cannot expect that he is going to drop everything for you, even if your father is the President of the Turkey!" the lady smirked.

Ayesha ignored her and focused on the woman in front of her. "Look, Ms…" Ayesha looked at the name badge that the woman was wearing, "Ms

Kara. I have something of great importance to discuss with Mr Demir that may concern this company. At least, would you please ask if he can see me for five minutes. It is about Mr Aksoy and '*The Seven*'."

Ayesha watched Ms Kara struggle with a moment of indecision before she picked up her phone and dialled a number. The woman had a short conversation in Turkish with the person on the other end of the line before putting the phone down.

The woman looked at Ayesha and said, "Mr Demir will give you five minutes. Go up to the eleventh floor and someone will meet you at the lift when you get there."

Ayesha thanked the woman and made her way to the right side of the foyer where she found six lifts in a spacious marble enclave. It was not long before one of the lifts opened and Ayesha took it to the eleventh floor.

At the eleventh floor, Ayesha was greeted by a man who introduced himself as Mr Demir's personal assistant. He led her out of the lift enclave into a carpeted lounge area from where Ayesha could see a large glass office on one side of the lounge. On the other side of the lounge Ayesha could see the entrance to a long corridor. It looked as if the corridor led to other offices on the floor. The man led Ayesha to the glass office and said, "This is Mr Demir's office. He will be with you in a moment. Take a seat and please do not touch anything."

Ayesha said, "Of course. Thank you."

Ayesha had just enough time to admire the expansive view of the city from Mr Demir's office windows before a handsome man in his forties wearing a sharp suit walked in. He abruptly greeted Ayesha in perfect English without smiling, and sat at his desk. "So Miss Dean, what do you know about Bilal Aksoy and '*The Seven*?"

Ayesha started, "Well actually I was hoping that you may be able to tell me a little more about Bilal Aksoy…" While she was speaking Ayesha secretly thought, "I've already learned something new! Mr Aksoy's name was Bilal, and the person who signed the note signed it with a 'B' too!"

Ayesha continued, "I am trying to help him and…"

At this Mr Demir immediately became upset, "Help him? He is dead! Who are you to come here and poke around other people's business? Miss Dean, I don't know who you are or why you are asking about '*The Seven*'. The only reason I agreed to see you today was to tell you to stop getting involved. You should not be looking into things that do not concern you. Why are you doing this?"

Ayesha calmly responded, "Mr Demir, I am not trying to hurt anyone. I am visiting from Australia and am just trying to fulfil a man's last wishes…"

Mr Demir cut in, "Whatever you are trying to do, I strongly advise you to stop. For your own sake. If you are on holiday, go see the sights, go shopping. Do not get involved in AKSOY or '*The Seven*' or whatever it is that you think you are doing."

He stood up. "Unfortunately I do not have further time for this. Please do as I say and don't get involved in looking for '*The Seven*'. It is dead and buried, like Mr Aksoy. You know where to exit." Mr Demir gestured towards the door.

Ayesha stood up to leave and said, "Thank you for your time. I didn't mean to cause any offence. I'm sorry to have troubled you."

Mr Demir nodded at Ayesha, then immediately sat down and focused his attention on his computer, dismissing her completely.

"Wow, what a rude man," Ayesha thought. "Talk about being stressed out!"

Ayesha left Mr Demir's office and thought she would tell the assistant that she was leaving, but she found nobody in the lounge area. She wondered why Mr Demir was so keen on her not finding out about '*The Seven*', and why he even agreed to see her in the first place.

Ayesha thought, "Surely he must think there is something significant about '*The Seven*'. He knows *something* about it because he spoke about it as if he knew it existed. Is he trying to hide something? And why?" Ayesha pondered.

As Ayesha was making her way to the lift area, a cleaner came out of the lifts wheeling a cleaning cart. He pushed the cart in Ayesha's direction and Ayesha absently nodded and smiled at him. He nodded back, but didn't bother smiling.

Walking slowly, and looking as if she were lost in thought, Ayesha noticed that the cleaner had pushed his cart almost to the point where Mr

Demir's office began. The cleaner then stopped, selected some cleaning items from the cart, and took the cleaning items into the bathrooms which were nearby.

At that moment Ayesha heard a raised voice coming from Mr Demir's office. She ducked down behind the cleaning cart so that she could hear more clearly. From her vantage point, Ayesha could just see the outline of Mr Demir and his assistant standing in the office. Mr Demir was angrily speaking loudly while the assistant was replying in a more subdued manner. They were speaking in Turkish but interlacing some English words.

As she was straining her ears trying to make out some of the words that were being spoken, Ayesha heard the soft ring of a bell signalling that a lift door was about to open. Wary of being caught eavesdropping, Ayesha quickly opened the door nearest to her and ducked inside. Ayesha found herself in a small, dark storage cupboard. There was some light coming from a low vent on one side of the room. However, other than the light coming from the vent, the room was in pitch darkness.

Inside the storage cupboard, Ayesha could hear the voices of Mr Demir and his assistant even more clearly. Ayesha realised that the vent opened straight into Mr Demir's office!

Mr Demir was talking now. She could still hear the agitation and anger in his voice, "He can't do this any longer. If he does not submit, he will be sorry!"

The milder voice of the assistant came through, "But Bilal Aksoy…"

Mr Demir cut in, "Bilal Aksoy was confused. At the end he was confused. Our actions are hampered every day and it is only getting worse."

The voices started moving away and then in a few moments, the voices sounded like they were coming closer. Ayesha sensed that the men had come out of the office and were now standing right outside the door of the storage cupboard. She held her breath. Just outside the door, Ayesha heard the assistant say, "You can raise it at the meeting."

Ayesha then heard the soft bell of the lift, and then the voices were gone. "Phew!" Ayesha thought. "That sounded like they were coming into the storage cupboard. But I guess I didn't really need to be worried that Mr Demir would come into the storage cupboard," she laughed to herself.

Ayesha listened out for any further noises. Hearing nothing, she quietly pulled down on the door handle to open the door. Nothing happened. She tried again, this time with more force. Again, the door handle did not move. Ayesha realised that she was locked inside!

CHAPTER TEN

"*Ya Allah,* please help me get out of here," Ayesha prayed as she tried the door handle one more time. "Nope. That door is not budging," she thought. Ayesha used her hands to feel around the edges of the door frame and found the light switch. Flicking the switch, she enjoyed about ten seconds of light before the single bulb flickered and slowly died, leaving her in darkness once again.

"Oh great. Just what I need," she softly muttered.

Ayesha took her smart phone out of her bag

and used the light from it to survey her surroundings in the darkness. The room was about two metres by two metres. There was horizontal shelving along three of the walls, except in the area just next to the door where there was a small recess where the shelving ended. In this recess, Ayesha saw that some larger cleaning items, such as several mops and a vacuum cleaner, were stored against the wall. The shelving on the other walls contained all sorts of office supplies, including toilet paper, paper towels, and hand towels.

Ayesha was heartened when she saw the bathroom supplies because she reasoned that the cleaner would need to come into the store room to restock the bathrooms. Ayesha had done plenty of work experience at Uncle Dave's law firm in a large building like this one. She was confident that office workers used a lot of paper towelling every day and the towelling dispensers in the bathrooms would most likely need to be refilled.

Ayesha examined the recess next to the door where the mops were kept. "I could squeeze in there," Ayesha thought, "and then when the cleaner comes to restock, I could try to sneak past him or somehow jam the door so that it doesn't lock behind him."

Ayesha took off her heels and put them into her tote bag. She then gently pulled the headband that she was wearing under her hijab, down around her neck. Holding down her hijab with one hand, she manoeuvred the headband off her head. After that, she squeezed herself into the small recess next to the door and pulled the curtain across the recess so that she would be hidden if anyone entered. She was very hopeful that the cleaner would come in for some bathroom supplies.

As she was waiting, Ayesha used her phone to text Sara.

"*Sara, I'm stuck in a storage cupboard.*

Will be out soon inshAllah.

Meet u in just over half hour, maybe 45 mins.

Please order me a meat pide. Yum."

She then made sure her phone was on silent.

"Oh no," thought Ayesha, "I shouldn't have started thinking about a meat *pide*."

Sara immediately texted back.

"What the…?

Storage cupboard?

OK will order for you."

Ayesha then heard what sounded like the bathroom door nearby opening and closing. She quickly scrunched up the headband that she held in her hand. The next moment, she heard a man in the foyer area humming an off-key tune. "Was that the cleaner?" Ayesha thought. She strained her ears. The humming man was coming closer. Ayesha calmed her breathing and made sure that the curtain was pulled across her.

It sounded like the humming man was moving

closer to where Ayesha last saw the cleaning cart. "It must be him," she thought. Ayesha heard the man moving some items around on the cart before walking towards the storage cupboard door. Ayesha tensed. The cleaner opened the door and tried to turn the light on. He muttered something in annoyance when he found out that the light bulb was dead.

He opened the door wider and Ayesha sensed him bending down towards the floor. She assumed that he had put a door stopper under the door, as the door remained open when he went out towards the cart again.

Ayesha stayed where she was behind the curtain. Ten seconds later the cleaner was back inside the storage cupboard. Ayesha sensed that he was picking up some of the bathroom supplies from the back wall.

She quietly pulled the curtain back a little bit so

that she could see what the cleaner was doing. The light coming in from the doorway made it easy for Ayesha to see the inside of the room quite clearly. Ayesha saw that the cleaner was facing the back wall, with his back towards her.

"He is too close," Ayesha thought. "If I try to manoeuvre out of this awkward position and creep out the door he will surely hear and see me, and then report me to security."

Instead Ayesha took the scrunched-up headband in her hand and stealthily eased her arm out of the curtain, making sure that the cleaner still had his back towards her. Ayesha reached out and stuffed her headband into the small space where the door's latch would fit into the door frame, and prayed that it would hold in place. Using her fingers she made sure that the headband was securely in place, then she gently pulled her arm back behind the curtain.

A few seconds later the cleaner turned around

with an armful of paper towels and took them to his cart. Shortly after that, he pulled the door stop out from underneath the door and let the door close shut on its own. He did not bother to check if the door had latched properly as the storage cupboard was not a secure area.

Ayesha waited until she heard the cart rolling towards the lifts, and heard the cleaner take the lift to another floor. She then pulled the door open and breathed a deep breath. "*Alhamdulillah*," she thought as the door easily opened towards her. The door had not latched as her headband was blocking the latch.

Once out of the storage cupboard, Ayesha pulled out her headband from the door frame and stuffed it into her bag. She then put her heels back on as she waited for the next lift. "Hopefully, Mr Demir doesn't come back from his meeting just now," she thought. Ayesha breathed a sigh of relief when she saw that there was nobody in the next lift and she could exit the building without incident.

***

Jess and Sara were sitting at an outside table at a picturesque terrace café overlooking the Hagia Sophia when Ayesha approached them with a smile of relief on her face. Jess called out, "Just in time, the food has only just arrived. We also ordered you a mint tea in these cute tiny tea glasses."

"Ah, thank you!" Ayesha exclaimed as she sat down to enjoy her lunch.

"Glad to see you got out of the storage cupboard Ayesh!" Sara exclaimed.

"Yeah, that was a minor hiccough," Ayesha laughed good-naturedly. "So, I didn't get very far with the CEO of AKSOY, Mr Demir. Other than finding out that Mr Aksoy's name is Bilal, which fits in nicely with the theory that B.Ev is Mr Bilal Aksoy."

"That's useful, Ayesh!" said Jess. "I asked Mrs

Nurhan to help me search the local white pages for any people with the last name Ev. We only found a few, so Mrs Nurhan helped to call them and find out whether there were any people starting with 'B' in their family. There were none. By the way, those calls have been added to our room charge."

"No worries, Jess, thanks for that. So I guess we can safely say that Bilal Aksoy is the same B.Ev of the hidden note," said Ayesha. "I mean, it makes sense given that the book of maps with the hidden note came from Mr Aksoy's house. He's also the founder of a large building company, and his name is Bilal. Perhaps he likes going by the name Ev because of his building company, or maybe it's a nickname."

"Yeah, who knows," agreed Sara. "I think you're right though, B.Ev is most probably Bilal Aksoy. It's good we've come that far because I went around to four different major banks this morning and none of them had any safety deposit boxes that matched up with our key. So I have nothing helpful to report."

"At least we know not to go back to any of those banks!" responded Ayesha. "Perhaps Emre or Mehmet can give us some ideas about what that key might open."

The girls finished their meal and started making their way towards the tram to take them to Mehmet's shop in the Old Bazaar. As the girls left the terrace café, a man at a nearby table wearing a baseball cap and sunglasses also got up to leave and began following them.

**

It was a five-minute walk from the closest tram stop to the Old Book Bazaar. As the day was pleasant and sunny, the girls found that they had to dodge and weave around plenty of tourists who were excitedly walking around the area and seeing the sites.

Once they had taken several turns towards their destination, Ayesha began having the uneasy sense that someone was following them. Every time she turned her head to figure out which direction they should be going, a male figure seemed to jump out of her line of vision and blend in with the crowd. Ayesha noticed that it happened to be the same male figure every time.

From the corner of her eye she could see that he was wearing a blue baseball cap, but she had not been able to get a good look at him. "Perhaps I'm just being paranoid," Ayesha thought. "I won't tell the others until I know for sure that we're being followed."

The girls turned into the entrance to the Grand Bazaar and started making their way to the courtyard of the Old Book Bazaar. Once inside the markets, the girls were surrounded on all sides by the crowds of shoppers and their progress became a lot slower. At one stage, Sara could not go past a stall selling beautiful embroidered cushion covers, so the friends stopped for her to make the purchase. At the stall next door, Ayesha noticed a pair of unique black and gold moccasin-style shoes that would work well with what she was wearing. Her peach-coloured high heels were starting to become uncomfortable with all the walking they had to do. Ayesha bargained with the seller to achieve a reasonable price and paid for the attractive moccasins, which she put on straight away.

Once the girls had finished their purchases, Ayesha quickly glanced behind her to see if she could still see the man in the blue cap, but all she saw was a colourful sea of fellow shoppers.

"What's wrong, Ayesh?" Jess asked.

"Nothing for the moment," Ayesha replied. "I thought there may have been someone following us, but I'm not sure. If he was following us though, he doesn't seem to be around anymore."

The friends moved on and finally arrived at Mehmet's shop. However, they were surprised to see that the store appeared to be closed, even though it was a business day. Ayesha peered closely through the glass window of the shop and could see that the light was on in the back room, so she knocked on the door.

A few moments later, Emre opened the door and let the girls in. Ayesha noticed that his face was lined with worry. "What happened?" Ayesha asked. "Is everything ok?"

"The shop was broken into last night!" Emre responded.

CHAPTER ELEVEN

Emre carefully closed and locked the front door after letting the others in. "My poor father is so upset," he continued. "The back room is a mess. Thankfully whoever broke in left the front room as it was. I think the intruders must have known *exactly* what they were looking for and where to find it. They only concentrated on the back room!"

"Oh I'm so sorry!" said Ayesha. "What a horrible thing to have happened." She followed Emre into the back room of the shop where she saw Mehmet bending down to observe some of the damage that had been done. The room looked like a disaster. Hundreds of Mehmet's precious books and manuscripts were strewn all over the ground. Ayesha could see that many of the ancient pages had been torn and stepped on.

Ayesha noticed that all the books that were in the glass display cabinets were untouched. Instead, whoever had broken in had rifled through the many boxes that were on the ground.

"Mehmet, I'm so sorry, this is terrible," Ayesha said as she helped Mehmet to stand from his crouched position on the floor. Sara and Jess gingerly stepped over some items blocking the doorway, and squeezed past two damaged boxes, before coming to stand next to Ayesha to survey the room. Sara asked, "Have you called the police yet?"

"Yes, I've called them," said Emre. "They are

on their way."

"Good," said Ayesha. "It's probably a good idea if you leave everything in place for the moment. The police may be able to find some evidence that will lead to whoever was responsible for this. Do you know if anything was stolen?"

Mehmet shook his head, "I have not checked everything yet. But my most valuable manuscripts have not been touched. It looks like they were looking for something in this room."

"But in the meantime, they didn't care what they destroyed along the way," added Emre sadly. Looking down near a box by her feet, Ayesha noticed a mark on one of the torn manuscripts nearby. Someone had left a muddy shoeprint behind! Ayesha made a mental note to let the police know about it. She used her phone to take a picture of the shoeprint to remind herself. "It looks like this intruder wore some shoes with a bit of grip," Ayesha thought, as she put her phone back into her bag.

Just then, Ayesha looked up and saw that someone was peering into the front of the shop. Ayesha didn't have a clear view of the person, but she could just see that he appeared to be wearing a blue cap. Ayesha immediately craned her neck to peer around Sara, in order to get a better view. Whoever was looking in had now disappeared. "Oh no you don't," Ayesha muttered as she passed her bag to Jess. "I'll be back in ten minutes," she called as she rushed out of the door.

Once she was in the courtyard, Ayesha found herself among a throng of shoppers who all seemed to be out and about in the sunshine. She looked to her right and couldn't see anything of interest. She looked to her left and saw a male wearing a blue cap walking briskly in the other direction, about fifty metres away from her.

Ayesha began running towards him, but it was

difficult to move quickly as she kept getting stuck behind browsing shoppers. "Excuse me! Excuse me!" she said as she weaved her way through the crowd. The man seemed to be getting further and further away from her when she saw him turn towards the right, into a busy street outside of the market grounds.

Ayesha continued pushing her way through the crowd until she too reached the outside street and began sprinting. It was not so crowded outside of the market place and Ayesha gained some good ground running in the same direction that she had seen the man take. After about half a minute, Ayesha caught sight of him again. He was about seventy metres away now and running left into another street further ahead. "Come on Ayesha, not too far away now, you can do it," she told herself.

Ayesha caught up to the street that she had seen the man turn left into and then slowed down.

She surveyed all the people walking in the street, but could not see the man anywhere. There were some non-descript buildings lining both sides of the street. Not far ahead though, Ayesha observed a gathering of people entering a building that had a sign in front of it. "Hmmm," she thought. "He might have gone in there. It seems to be open to the public."

Ayesha ran up to the building and read that it was the entry to the Basilica Cistern. She walked into the small office space within the building and saw that several ticket counters were open at the reception. After quickly buying a ticket, Ayesha went through a large doorway and found herself descending a long, dimly lit, wooden stairway. Unfortunately the stairway was full of tourists who seemed to be moving extremely slowly.

Ayesha looked around and realised that she was actually underground in a huge, dark, cavernous space that was built with rows and rows of ancient Roman columns and archways as far as the eye could see. Ayesha could not see the bottom of the Roman columns as they were all under water. She had no idea how deep the water was as she could not see beneath the surface due to the darkness of the cavern. Lights had been placed on the main Roman columns at a point just above the surface of the water to provide some light and to highlight the spectacular ancient Roman structure.

It appeared that the stairway led on to wooden walkways that were built over the water to allow tourists to explore the cavern. Up ahead, Ayesha noticed that there was some sort of commotion among the crowd. Ayesha stood on her tiptoes to see over the shoulder of the person in front of her. She saw that a man with a hat was pushing his way through the crowd about thirty metres away from her. "That might be him," she thought as she accidently walked into the person in front of her.

Ayesha's heart sank as she considered that the whole stairway was filled with tourists and visitors to the site. If she was going to catch up to the man, she would need to push her way through the large line of people.

Just then, Ayesha felt a small opening within the crowd in front of her and used it as an opportunity to push forward. "I'm sorry, please excuse me, I have lost someone up ahead and I need to reach them as soon as possible!" she apologised as she tried to manoeuvre her way through the crowd. She had only moved a few feet forward when she was stopped by a person coming in the opposite direction.

"Hello, Miss Ayesha," she heard the slow, croaky voice of Berke, the creepy librarian, as he blocked her path. "Very nice to see you again," he added without smiling.

"Oh. Hello," Ayesha automatically said, while

craning her neck to see where the man in the cap had gone. However, every time Ayesha tried to look past him, Berke annoyingly shifted his body so that he was directly in front of her. "Why are you in such a hurry?" he asked.

Ayesha sighed as she lost sight of the man in the cap who had disappeared into the darkness of the huge cistern. Although the stairs seemed to be leading into one path causing a bottle-neck for the tourists, Ayesha could see that there were many built wooden paths all over the cistern. The man may have taken any number of paths and if it was one of the less populated ones, Ayesha didn't want to be caught alone with him in a dark place, surrounded by water on all sides.

"Oh it's nothing," responded Ayesha. "I guess you are not working at the library today?"

"I like to get out and have fun sometimes too, Miss Ayesha," he said.

Ayesha felt his reptilian eyes studying her

intensely. He continued, "Have you found out anything more about '*The Awrad*'?"

Ayesha started turning around towards the exit. "This guy is way too interested," she thought. She called casually over her shoulder, "No, no, I've just been having a nice time seeing the sights. Oh well, I must be off now. Bye!"

"Wait!" called Berke as Ayesha rushed towards the exit. "Emina says she wants you to visit her again at the library. She says it's very, very important and you *must* bring the note!"

Ayesha kept going and pretended she didn't hear him. "Oh no! He must have overheard us talking about the note at the library," she thought to herself. She couldn't help shuddering. "That guy sure gives me the creeps."

***

Appreciating the sunshine on her face outside, Ayesha ran back to Mehmet's shop. She hoped that the others were not too worried about her. As she approached the shop she could see that a couple of police vehicles were parked nearby, and some police officers were coming in and out of the shop. She found her friends seated on a bench not far from Mehmet's shop. "Oh Ayesha, there you are!" exclaimed Jess. "What happened?"

"The person who I thought was following us on our way to the shop was a man in a blue cap. Then while we were inside Mehmet's shop, I saw, out of the corner of my eye, a figure in a cap peeping in," Ayesha explained. "He is definitely suspicious. I just wanted to get a good look at him really, so that we might be able to describe him to police if need be. Unfortunately, I couldn't get close enough to him to see his features. I know he moved pretty quickly, and his physique was rather fit. But I couldn't say anything more, except that he wore a blue cap, jeans, and a dark top."

"Oh, what a bummer. It was a good try

though," said Sara. "I wasn't too worried about you, knowing you could kick butt if need be. But poor Emre was pretty worried when you ran off. He wanted to go after you, but needed to stay with his dad. They are still inside the shop with the police."

Ayesha walked into Mehmet's shop to find Emre. She saw a number of police officers standing around. A couple of officers were speaking separately to Mehmet and Emre, and a crime scene officer was dusting for fingerprints at the back door. One officer approached Ayesha and said she was not allowed to enter the back room.

"Yes, of course, I understand," replied Ayesha. "My name is Ayesha Dean, I am a friend of Mehmet and Emre and was here earlier before you arrived. I just wanted to let an officer know that I saw a shoe mark on one of the manuscripts on the floor near the north-east corner of that back room.

It's behind one of the boxes."

"OK, thank you," replied the officer. "I'll make sure we look for it. We might need a statement from you too, Miss, if anything was moved before we got here."

"Sure," said Ayesha.

Ayesha exchanged contact details with the officer who told her his name was Sergeant Omer. She also informed him that she thought that someone may have been following her earlier, but she couldn't provide any further details. Sergeant Omer warned Ayesha to generally be careful as some tourists have had their belongings stolen by pickpockets in the past.

After speaking to the Sergeant, Ayesha looked around for Emre. He had just finished speaking to an officer and came out to the front of the shop to meet Ayesha.

"The police found some fingerprints at the back door," Emre said. "I also saw them take photos of the shoe print. They said they would run some searches on the fingerprints to see if they matched anyone on their database. But unfortunately, they don't have any other leads as yet. They are going to ask around the other shop owners for any potential witnesses, but I'm not getting my hopes up."

"Hey, I'm sorry for your dad," Ayesha said sympathetically. "I wonder if this is related to the book of maps and the note at all. I have a feeling there's definite interest in the hidden note, and unfortunately the fact that it was found in a book in your father's bookstore is not a secret."

"You could be right," agreed Emre. "I just don't understand why people have to be so destructive, though. It wasn't enough for them to break in and try and steal, they had to destroy all those other books and manuscripts as well."

Emre looked at Ayesha and smiled, "Well, at

least we can be thankful that you are OK. I was worried about you when you ran off so fast!"

Ayesha smiled, "Yes, I'm OK. I saw a suspicious man looking into the shop who I thought was following me earlier, but I wasn't able to get a decent look at him. Oh well, it was a good try!"

After the police had left the shop, Emre kindly drove Ayesha, Sara, and Jess back to their hotel. It had been a long day and Ayesha was looking forward to a quick hotel meal, and a relaxing soak in the hotel room's jet spa bath. When the girls entered the lobby, Mrs Nurhan called them over to her desk.

"Ayesha, Ayesha come over here," Mrs Nurhan frantically waved them over. "Were you expecting a male guest today?"

"No!" said Ayesha in puzzlement.

Mrs Nurhan continued, "I didn't think so dear. Well today I saw a man snooping around the rooms and I walked up to him and demanded what he was doing! Well, the sight of him! No sleeves, and tattoos all over his body!"

The girls smiled at Mrs Nurhan's shock and horror at the tattoos. Perhaps she wasn't used to tattooed clientele, but it seemed to Ayesha that tattoos were far more common these days. Whatever people said about them, as an aspiring detective, Ayesha thought that tattoos could be useful for helping to identify a person or suspect, although she wouldn't want one herself.

"Well!" Mrs Nurhan continued. "The man was very rude and did not take kindly to me asking him what he was doing, even though it is *my* hotel! Anyway, he would not tell me what he was doing, but he said he was looking for Ayesha Dean and that he wanted to talk to you!"

Mrs Nurhan put on a stern face as she addressed Ayesha. "Ayesha, my dear, I'm sure you are old enough to know who you should be keeping company with. But I would have thought you would be very wary about being in company with a man like that!"

Later that night, Ayesha closed her eyes and relaxed as she tried to sleep. She could hear the soft breathing of Sara and Jess in the other two single beds within the room. A peaceful, hot bath had taken away any last sting of annoyance that Ayesha had felt at Mrs Nurhan's warning. While the older lady had helpfully told her about the male visitor, her superior and judgemental manner had been a little irritating. Ayesha remembered that it was always better to exercise patience with those types of people, and she had kindly thanked Mrs Nurhan for the information and advice before heading back to the hotel room.

Just as Ayesha was about to drift off to sleep, she heard the unmistakeable soft click of a door latch. Keeping very still, Ayesha opened her eyes in the darkness to see the hotel room door slowly opening. Someone was entering the room. It was a masked figure covered in black!

CHAPTER TWELVE

Seeing that the black figure was now inside their room, Ayesha wondered whether she should shout out straight away or pretend to be having a bad dream and hopefully scare the person away without risking the person feeling trapped and doing something rash.

The male figure seemed to be moving very slowly in the darkness and heading towards the direction of the hotel safe. Ayesha thought that her eyes must have been more accustomed to the darkness inside the room than the stranger's, because he seemed to be awkwardly feeling the air in front of him as if he couldn't see where he was going.

Ayesha looked towards Jess's bed, which was placed in the way of the kitchen area where the safe was kept. The intruder did not realise that there was an extra single bed in the room and he bumped into Jess's bed quite forcefully and stubbed his toe. On feeling the impact from the bump, Jess woke up and saw the black masked figure standing over her. Jess immediately started screaming!

Ayesha heard the intruder mutter, "Oww!" before he turned around and ran out of the room. Ayesha grabbed her hoodie by the side of the bed and yanked it on while she got up to go after the intruder. Pulling the hood over her head while she ran out of the hotel into the street, Ayesha saw the humour in worrying about her hijab on this chase rather than remembering to put on some shoes, which would have been a lot more helpful.

After running in bare feet for another twenty metres or so, Ayesha slowed down as she had already lost sight of the masked figure as soon as he had left the room. He could have disappeared into any of the dark, narrow streets around the area and Ayesha would have little chance of finding him in the darkness. She walked quickly back to the hotel so that she could report the incident to her uncle and the police.

The next morning, Ayesha and her friends were seated in the breakfast room with Uncle Dave and Mr Isa. The police had come and gone, and unfortunately none of the girls were able to describe much more of the intruder other than that he wore black clothes, a black balaclava mask with eye holes, and that he had a man's build. Ayesha added that she had heard that the intruder had a male voice when he had muttered "Oww!" before leaving, but she hadn't caught the man's accent.

Ayesha told the police that the intruder had run away before he had any chance of stealing anything.

"OK, from now on," Uncle Dave was saying, "Whenever you are in the hotel room, you have to use the additional latch. One lock on the door handle is not enough!"

Ayesha briefly got up to place a kiss on Uncle Dave's worried brow. "We will be much more vigilant from now on Day!" She added, "I usually check the door latch, but I guess I must have forgotten last night. Luckily *alhamdulillah* we are all OK."

"Yes. Lucky," agreed Uncle Dave. "So where are you all now with your investigation? Obviously things seem to be getting more serious."

"Yes, it does seem to be getting serious," Ayesha agreed. "Although a lot of things don't seem to be adding up at the moment." She explained further, "Yesterday there was a man in a blue cap who was following us around, but then when I started following him, he seemed to want to get away from me. Then when I was almost close enough to see what the man looked like…Berke, the strange librarian shows up out of nowhere and blocks my path!"

"Do you think Berke is connected with the man in the blue cap?" Jess asked.

Sara pointed out, "Remember how keen Berke was to find out what you knew about the *Awrad-al-Usbu,* Ayesh. Perhaps he had someone follow you to see if you were on the trail?"

"You could be right," said Ayesha. "But I'm also wondering about the man that Mrs Nurhan saw loitering about yesterday."

"The man with the tattoos?" asked Jess.

"Sounds to me like the scary supplier Arslan might have paid us a little visit," Sara commented.

"Do you think he was the person who also broke in?" asked Uncle Dave. "I still marvel at how you manage to find all of these people, Ayesha," he said good-naturedly.

"It could have been Arslan who broke into our room, I guess," said Ayesha. "But why did he come earlier in the daytime when Mrs Nurhan was around to see him? Surely if he was going to break in he wouldn't want to obviously raise suspicion," Ayesha reasoned.

"Perhaps," Uncle Dave mused. "So do you think it was that librarian you talked about who broke in?" he asked.

"It could be," Ayesha guessed. "I guess it could be any one of them, including the guy in the blue cap. I also wonder about the person who broke into Mehmet's shop and whether that is connected to all of this."

"What? There's been another break-in?" Mr Isa spoke up incredulously.

Sara responded, "Yes Dad, it was the shop of

one of our friends, but thankfully nothing major was stolen."

Mr Isa looked at her in a concerned manner, "You make sure to stay safe OK? Stick together."

"We'll be OK thanks Dad," Sara replied.

The group resumed eating breakfast, each in their own thoughts as to who may have been the intruder and why. After a while it was time for the men to leave for their conference.

"Well, I trust that you have everything under control." Uncle Dave got up and kissed Ayesha on the forehead.

"We sure do, *inshAllah*," said Ayesha.

"Our conference will finish up in a couple of days," said Uncle Dave. "Then we can spend the next three or four days seeing the sights and eating together! I can't wait for the break. In the meantime, please make sure you stay safe, and keep to well-populated areas. Please always be aware of your surroundings. I'm worried about this intruder on the loose."

Ayesha reassured her uncle and told him not to worry.

He shook his head and said, "Impossible, of course I worry. But I also know you have a strong head on your shoulders! OK, take care. You know where to reach me," he reminded Ayesha. The two men then said goodbye and left for their conference.

The three friends finished off their breakfast and went to their room to freshen up. Once inside the room, Ayesha walked over to the safe to check on the key. She had been thinking about why the intruder had broken into their hotel room. He might have been a random burglar, or he might have intentionally targeted their room because he was looking for something in particular. Given that she had been followed in a suspicious way the other day, Ayesha tended to think that the intruder knew what he was looking for.

Ayesha took another look at the room safe. It was a rather small safe, just a little bigger than a shoebox. Ayesha tried to move it and noticed that, while it was heavy, it was not actually attached to anything in the room. She thought that someone could possibly come in and carry the whole safe away if they wanted to.

Ayesha shook her head. She didn't think it was a good idea to leave the hidden key in the safe now that they knew someone had already broken into the room rather easily. Ayesha took off her chain bracelet and threaded it through the little key that she had taken out of the safe. She then re-attached her bracelet with the little key around her wrist.

"Just letting you know, guys," Ayesha announced to the others, "I've got the key attached to me now. Just in case someone breaks in while we are away…"

"Oh no, hey guys," Jess interrupted as she was

looking down at her phone. "My aunty is in hospital. I've just got this text from Mum. I'll have to bail out this morning and call home."

"Oh sorry, Jess. Bad news," Ayesha said sympathetically. "Hey, you better hang around in the hotel common areas while we're away. You know, just in case our intruder decides to return."

"Yeah, thanks Ayesh, I will," said Jess.

Ayesha and Sara finished getting ready to go out for the day. Ayesha dressed herself in a pair of royal-blue capri pants with a soft white linen top that was styled in an interesting diagonal shape across the front of her thighs. Her bright pink hijab was pulled to the back and styled in the shape of a bun above her neck. Some funky earrings, a chunky silver necklace, and the new moccasins that she bought from the Bazaar completed her outfit.

The previous evening, before they had gone to sleep, Ayesha had asked Sara to send Emre the photo she had taken of the key. Emre had shown his father the photo of the key and Mehmet immediately recognised that it was the type of key used by Turkish banks for their safety deposit boxes.

Emre then emailed Ayesha a list of four of the largest banks in Istanbul that were known to keep safety deposit boxes for their clients. None of these banks were on the list of those that Sara had already checked out. The girls were planning on visiting those banks today.

As Ayesha and Sara were passing the front desk, Mrs Nurhan called them over to her. "Ayesha! I am sorry you had a bad experience with the intruder last night. Please be assured this has never happened in my hotel before. It is very bad luck. You should have locked your door properly!" she chided, not wanting any of the blame to be placed on her hotel.

Ayesha let the words roll over her. She thought

Mrs Nurhan was a harmless enough woman, even though the matron appeared to have the type of personality that could not resist taking a subtle jab at other people.

Mrs Nurhan continued, "You seem to be a very popular girl, Ayesha. I have received an email this morning from a staff member at the Suleymaniye Library, a person by the name of Emina, who says that she needs to speak with you urgently about a note. She writes that she will wait for you at the library this morning."

Mrs Nurhan looked up at Ayesha in a calculating manner, "Well, whatever that is about, it seems important! I have not ever had so many strange things happening at this hotel before. First the man with the tattoos, and then the intruder. Trouble, trouble." She tutted under her breath, and then turned her attention to Sara, studying her face for several moments before casually exclaiming,

"OK that's all. Have a nice day!"

Sara raised her eyebrows at Ayesha as they left the hotel, "She's a strange one that Mrs Nurhan!" Ayesha just smiled and said, "Yeah, but she's harmless. She likes to know everybody's business. Someone my aunt would call 'a real busy-body', but I think that she is a good person at heart."

Once they reached the taxi stand, Ayesha turned to Sara and asked, "Hey Sar, are you OK to go to the banks by yourself today? I should probably go and check out what Emina's message was all about from the library."

"Yeah sure," responded Sara. "I think it's a good idea we get this done today and hopefully we'll have time to make our day trip out to the Roman ruins either tomorrow or the next day."
"Fantastic, yeah, that would be fab! We can also meet up for lunch later," replied Ayesha.

The girls hugged goodbye and got into their respective taxis. Ayesha asked her taxi driver to take her to the Suleymaniye Library. On the way there, Ayesha again wondered what Emina would have to say to her that was so important about the note. "Perhaps she has found out more information about *'The Seven'*, or some kind of clue as to its location," Ayesha thought.

When she arrived at the Suleymaniye Library, Ayesha noticed that Emina was not at the front desk. Instead, she encountered Berke, who immediately said, "Miss Dean. I am very glad you are here. Emina was wanting to speak to you". He continued, "Come this way, she is waiting for you in her office."

Ayesha thought it strange that Emina was not at the front desk to greet her herself. There was something suspicious in the way that Berke was being so friendly and helpful in assisting Ayesha to meet up with Emina. Ayesha did not trust Berke, and his creepy vibe was noticeable in the way he had greeted her today. Ayesha decided to follow him to see what he was up to, but she paid attention to her instincts, which were telling her to be wary.

Berke led her into a very long corridor behind the front desk. They passed several closed doors and made a right-hand turn down another corridor before coming to an open door right at the end of the passageway. Berke stepped aside and indicated for Ayesha to enter.

Ayesha cautiously entered the room, which was a medium-sized office, set up with a desk and a couple of guest chairs. At the back of the office there was a closed door that appeared to lead somewhere else. There were also a few large, old-fashioned wooden wardrobes that Ayesha assumed contained files or books.

Berke indicated towards a guest seat and invited Ayesha to sit down. "I will go and let Emina know you are here, she will be here shortly," he said before leaving the room and closing the door behind him.

A few moments after Berke left the room, Ayesha heard a strange noise coming from one of the wardrobes in the room. From her seat, Ayesha strained her ears to hear more clearly. "Perhaps I was just imagining it," Ayesha thought.

As she was staring at the cupboard and concentrating on what she thought she heard, Ayesha heard the unmistakeable sound of something bumping or knocking the wooden door from inside the cupboard. There was also another strange noise that Ayesha could not quite recognise.

Ayesha got up from her seat and walked towards the wardrobe where the sound was coming from. The thumping sound from inside the wardrobe was getting louder and more insistent. Grabbing the handle of the wardrobe, Ayesha yanked the door open and screamed in shock when she found Emina staring at her with fear in her eyes. Emina's mouth had been taped up and her hands and feet had been bound with rags.

Still in shock, Ayesha looked around when she heard the sound of a key turning in the door. Berke had re-entered the room and was locking the door so that they had no means of escape. With him was a strong-looking man that Ayesha had never met before.

He was wearing a blue cap!

CHAPTER THIRTEEN

Ayesha stood facing the man in the blue cap. He was standing a metre away from Berke who was still by the door. The man was solidly built, had dark hair, and was of medium height. He looked to be in his early forties, and there was nothing unusual in his appearance. He wore casual clothes, but Ayesha could tell that his clothing was of good quality. From behind her, Ayesha could hear the muffled sound of Emina whimpering in fear from beneath the tape over her mouth.

"How am I going to get out of this situation?"

Ayesha wondered. "And how am I going to get Emina to safety? *Ya Allah*, please help me," she silently prayed.

Ayesha quickly considered her options. She thought it was best to do all that she could to negotiate calmly, and reason with her abductors as an initial tactic. In the short space of time that she had observed the man working together with Berke, it appeared to Ayesha that Berke was the inferior person in their relationship. Berke seemed to defer to the authority of the man in the cap with his body language and actions.

Ayesha decided to address the man in the blue cap, "So we finally meet face to face."

"Yes. Miss Dean, I presume?" he asked in a clear American accent.

She bowed her head slightly to acknowledge his comment, "And you are?"

"I am Yavuz Aksoy," he bowed gallantly as if he was some sort of knight in shining armour.

"So, to what do I owe the pleasure of this meeting?" she asked.

He smiled in a cagey manner, "I think you know, Miss Dean. I take it you are just as interested as I am in finding *'The Seven'*, are you not?"

Ayesha used her peripheral vision to see if there was anything she could use within the room to escape. She would need to make sure that nothing bad happened to Emina, who was still tied up, if she were to escape. Ayesha knew that there was another closed door in the room, but she didn't know whether it led anywhere or was just a storage cupboard. There were no other windows or openings to the room.

Ayesha responded calmly, "Perhaps I might be interested in finding *'The Seven'*. But only so that it can be restored to the place where its 'Keeper' intended for it to be...preserved in the library so that everyone may benefit from its wisdom and beauty."

"Oh, you do-gooders think you are so great!" Yavuz Aksoy responded with venom. "You've probably never been in the situation where you even had to *consider* the need for money. It grows on trees for you, doesn't it? Here you are travelling with your little friends on Daddy's holiday overseas, everything paid for. What do you know of hardship? If you really needed it, you would also try to get your hands on something of value to sell it and make some money."

Ayesha countered, "And I suppose you know of poverty? Being an heir to the well-known Aksoy Building Corporation with offices all over Turkey..."

He smirked at her, "You think my grandfather and uncle gave us an easy life? You think wrong, Miss Dean. My parents took me to America when I was a baby. My *wonderful* Aksoy family was not happy that my father married my mother, who was born into poverty and had become the family's maid. No, my mother was beautiful, but she wasn't good enough for my grandparents and they rejected her. My father left the family and took us to America with the little money that he had to his name. He never asked his family for money ever again, and it made me mad! Why should my uncle have received everything, and my father nothing!" he cried.

"No, it wasn't fair," he continued. "Life is not always fair dear Ayesha, and we can't go around judging people who do things because they need money," he said sadly.

As he was talking, Ayesha had slowly eased herself closer to the door. She didn't want to move too quickly because that would attract their attention. She saw that Berke was comfortably seated on a guest chair and had the door key carelessly dangling from a chain in his hand. If she could get to Berke, whom she thought looked weedy and a little weak, she could probably kick him in the groin and grab the key. Hopefully then she could quickly open the door before being overpowered by Yavuz Aksoy, who looked quite fit and strong.

Ayesha had to keep Yavuz talking and distracted, "So, did your uncle have any children?"

"No. I am the only heir to the great Bilal Aksoy," he announced.

"So if you are the only heir to the Aksoy fortune, why are you in need of money? I presume that you're looking for *'The Seven'* so that you can sell the manuscript?" Ayesha asked while slowly inching forward little by little.

"Bilal Aksoy didn't approve of what he called my 'Western ways'. Ha! As if everyone in the West is the same!" he explained. "So what if I like to drink alcohol and have lots of girlfriends? It was none of his business. I came back here six months before he died and lived with him, kept him company, put up with his nurses and doctors always coming to the house at all hours. I deserved taking the Mercedes out that day!" he exclaimed. "He shouldn't have been angry that I crashed it. What's it to him anyway? He was dying. I had only drunk a little bit. I wasn't *very* drunk. The stupid old lady should not have been walking so close to the road!"

Ayesha could hear in Yavuz's voice that he was getting worked up and upset. She hoped that he would calm down.

Yavuz looked thoughtfully into the distance and continued, "My uncle judged me and thought I couldn't run his company. He judged me, and didn't leave me anything in his will! Oh well, besides the fact that I can live in his house, he hasn't left me any money. How am I supposed to live? Instead, he left everything in the trust of that idiot Demir, who I despise. That suck-up. That 'know-it-all' Demir can't run the company without the clause hanging over his head."

"What clause?" Ayesha asked. Silently she thought, "I'm nearly at the door! It looks like Berke is still looking the other way!"

Yavuz continued, "Oh some legal clause in my uncle's will about thirty percent of shares in the company going to me if I fulfil certain conditions. Demir always has to worry about me because I could be the next major shareholder in the company." He laughed bitterly, "I really take too much pleasure in making things hard for him."

Yavuz was still contemplating his unfair life when Ayesha silently manoeuvred herself to within one metre from the key in Berke's hand. She silently made eye contact with Emina who nodded slightly, understanding what Ayesha intended to do. Emina started making as much noise as she could with her taped mouth and began struggling on the floor to get Yavuz's attention.

In that moment, Ayesha grabbed the key from Berke's hand, but the chain got stuck around his wrist. He immediately stood up from his chair and moved to grab Ayesha, but she kicked him hard and swiftly in his groin. He doubled up in pain and fell to the ground. Ayesha grabbed the door key, which had fallen on the floor, and rapidly turned around to see Yavuz's fist coming towards her face. She blocked the punch with her arm and countered it with a double punch to Yavuz's nose and stomach. Ayesha caught the site of blood at Yavuz's nose, but in the next moment he had somehow twisted Ayesha's arm behind her back so that she was held in an awkward position and she felt as if he would break her arm behind her back. She lifted her foot and stamped down as hard as she could on his foot behind hers. Yavuz yelped in pain as he dropped his hold on her arm, but

Ayesha turned around too late to miss a blow to the side of her head. The last thing she remembered was the worried look on Emina's face as Ayesha sank to the ground, and everything went black.

***

Ayesha woke up to find herself lying in the foot well of the backseat of a moving car. She had a rag tied around her mouth and her hands and feet were bound with rope-like material. Amazingly, she still seemed to have her hijab on although it was a little crooked. "I guess Yavuz still has some sort of respect," Ayesha thought. "Not much though it seems."

Ayesha tried to change her position because the partition between the seats was digging into her back. She must have made some noise because she saw Yavuz in the driver's seat look into the rear vision mirror before saying, "Oh, I was wondering when you were going to wake up!"

Ayesha groaned and tried to move her hands around. Her hands were bound very tightly in front of her torso. She started slowly working at moving her wrists to loosen the binding as much as she could, but they had been tied too tightly to make much of a difference.

Berke, who was in the front passenger seat turned around and gave Ayesha a death stare. He was obviously very angry about Ayesha's kick to his groin, which gave her a small feeling of justice given her current situation.

Yavuz spoke up, "Miss Dean, if you are wondering what happened to that little key that was around your wrist, you will be pleased to know that I now have it safe with me. It's a safety deposit key and I know which bank my uncle used to use."

Ayesha tried to talk but it was difficult with the rag in her mouth. She felt something digging into her hip. "Is that my phone? Yes, it is!" she thought excitedly. She slowly moved her hands towards her pants pocket and pressed a few buttons. In her position lying across the foot well she could not see what she was pressing. Ayesha just hoped that she had pressed the right button for recording. Thankfully the phone was on silent and nothing could be heard from it.

"What's that you say?" asked Yavuz Aksoy. "I can't hear you. You seem to have something in your mouth." He chuckled at his own joke and continued, "Are you asking why I know that was my uncle's key? Ha! Well you see, my uncle used to go on and on about *'The Seven'*. About how he was the *'Keeper of The Seven'* and that the librarians didn't know about it, but that it should now go back to the library and all that rubbish. I don't understand why he didn't just cash-in the overpriced pieces of paper! Manuscripts fetch hundreds of thousands of dollars as long as you know where to sell...and I've been doing my research. This Ibn Arabi manuscript is going to be worth a lot. There's some bad people that I owe some money to, and they're getting rather insistent that I come up with the cash."

Ayesha felt the car slow down and observed that Yavuz was driving into a building. Ayesha was comforted to see that it appeared that they were still somewhere in the city. They had passed several tall buildings on the way, so Ayesha was hopeful that Yavuz was not planning on killing her and dumping her body somewhere in the countryside. Yavuz drove the car into the underground car park of the building. The car park was completely deserted. He drove to the furthest corner of the car park and stopped the car.

"OK, Miss Dean," said Yavuz as he opened the door. He grabbed Ayesha under the shoulders and started dragging her out of the car. "This is where we say goodbye."

Ayesha noticed that Berke stayed where he was

in the car, but was anxiously looking over his shoulder, "Do you need some help, boss?" he asked Yavuz.

"You could have helped me earlier, you idiot," Yavuz replied annoyed. "I've already got her out now."

Yavuz had dragged Ayesha from the car and dumped her on the ground. She immediately sat up as best she could with her hands and feet tightly bound. Yavuz slowly crouched down so that he was face to face with Ayesha. "Miss Dean. It has been a pleasure. Thank you for kindly finding the key to unlock *'The Seven'* from their hiding place. I am sure that this is the key that I overheard my uncle muttering about before he died. I'm going to use it to get the manuscript out of its box and then you'll never hear from me again. Thankfully, as my uncle's next of kin, the bank will allow me to access the safety deposit box."

He slowly stood up, "As for you, Miss Dean.

As you can see we're in an abandoned car park. Nobody has used this building for years and years. Nobody ever comes down here. Only perhaps drug dealers and the type of unfriendly people who I owe money to. They would have no qualms in using you to their advantage. Nobody knows you are here, so you'll probably stay tied up for a while at least. It's unfortunate that such a pretty girl had to be involved this way. I had no choice you see, if I don't produce the money to these people in time, they said they're going to break my legs. Now, I don't want that to happen. You understand don't you, Miss Dean? As for your friend, the librarian…She served her purpose. It wasn't difficult to convince you to come and see what your sweet friend at the library had to say, was it? Unfortunately, she got wind that we wanted to lure you to the library and she had to try and warn you, didn't she? Silly girl. We had to keep her quiet, so she got what was coming to her."

Ayesha scowled at him, as she wasn't able to say anything with the rag tied around her mouth. Yavuz chuckled when he saw her expression. "Oh, she isn't hurt. Nothing more than a little scare, that's all. And we may have given her a little drug to shut her up when she wouldn't keep quiet after you foolishly tried to attack me," he said nonchalantly.

Yavuz turned away and started walking towards the car before stopping a few moments later. Turning his head back towards Ayesha he said, "Don't you worry about me, Miss Dean, I'll be long gone from this country before anybody ever finds out about what happened to you today."

Yavuz tipped his hat to her as a final farewell before getting into the car and driving away. Ayesha could see Berke smirking at her in the front passenger seat as they drove off. She watched the car drive away and took note of the local number plate, memorising the numbers so that she could report it to the police.

Ayesha then tried to move her arms and feet around and confirmed that the bindings were too tight for her to be able to loosen them without some sort of assistance. Looking around, she saw some scrap metal and rubbish dumped in one corner of the disused car park. Ayesha slowly stood up with her bound feet and jumped over to where she could see the piece of scrap metal. It took a while for Ayesha to make her way over to the other side of the vast empty car park. Her arms and legs were aching and she felt a bruise developing at the side of her cheek.

When she finally reached the corner, Ayesha made her way to one of the larger pieces of scrap metal that seemed to have relatively sharp edges. She began pressing the binding between her wrists over the sharp edge of the metal to try and cut the binding. After a good five minutes of solid effort, Ayesha had patiently managed to force the metal to cut through the bindings tying her hands together. She then quickly used her hands to untie the rag around her mouth, and the bindings at her feet.

Once she was untied Ayesha breathed a sigh of relief. "*Alhamdulillah*!" she exclaimed thankfully. "Now I have to get back and stop Yavuz from getting to the manuscript!"

CHAPTER FOURTEEN

Ayesha ran from the dark car park and blinked her eyes in the brightness outside. It appeared that the outside of this particular building was deserted, and the surrounding buildings were disused shopfronts in a bad state of disrepair. There were very few cars on the street and there was no one around.

She grabbed the phone out of her pocket and was dismayed to see that there was only one percent of charge left in the battery. She dialled the number of the local police and held the phone to her ear. Ayesha sighed in frustration when the phone battery went dead after just one dial tone.

She put the phone back into her pocket and was heartened to see that there were many tall buildings just a few blocks away. The sound of traffic in the near distance told Ayesha that she was still very much in the heart of the city. She just happened to be in a deserted block.

Ayesha ran towards the nearest buildings in order to call for help. She ran several blocks before reaching a main intersection. At the stop lights, Ayesha cried out in relief as she now knew where she was! On the other side of the main highway, Ayesha recognised the shiny silver-fronted building of the Aksoy offices. "*Alhamdulillah!*" she thought as she hurriedly crossed the road and entered the familiar lobby.

Inside the lobby, Ayesha quickly approached the ladies at the front desk and asked them to call the police. As one receptionist was dialling the police, Ayesha asked another to call Mr Demir down immediately, saying that it was an emergency involving Yavuz Aksoy.

Ayesha was handed the phone to police and she told them that she had been kidnapped. She recounted the names of her attackers and gave a description of their car and number plate. She asked the officer to inform Sergeant Omer of the situation, and to provide assistance to Emina, who had been attacked by the same offenders at the Suleymaniye Library.

As Ayesha finished her call to the police, she looked up to see a concerned Mr Demir before her. "Miss Dean! What has happened, are you OK?" he asked. "You look like you've been hurt!"

"Mr Demir!" Ayesha exclaimed, relieved to see a familiar face after her ordeal, even though they hadn't exactly parted as friends on the last occasion. "It's Yavuz Aksoy. He kidnapped me and now has the key I found when I followed the clues left by Bilal Aksoy. He's on his way to a safety deposit box, which I think might contain *'The Seven'*. We have to stop him!"

"Quick! Come with me," said Mr Demir as he led her out of the building towards the car park. "And please call me Adem."

"OK, and you can call me Ayesha," she replied.

"Are you sure you are OK?" he frowned at the bruise beginning to form on her cheek as they hurried to the car.

"I'm fine for now. I'll get a medical check-up later, but now we have to stop Yavuz from getting to the manuscript!"

They approached a dark blue, sporty-looking car parked in the staff car park. Adem clicked a small electronic device to automatically unlock the sleek vehicle. As Ayesha hurriedly slid into the passenger seat, she asked, "Which bank do you think he's heading towards?"

"I know which one," replied Adem as he pulled his seatbelt on. "It's one of the branches of AKbank in Istanbul, near Bilal Aksoy's old house. He always used that bank."

Adem expertly manoeuvred the vehicle out of the car park and began speeding along the highway. He pressed a button on the dashboard and within moments the voice of Sergeant Omer filled the interior of the cabin on speaker phone.

Ayesha exclaimed, "Sergeant Omer! We need your help! Yavuz Aksoy kidnapped me and stole a key. He's heading to a safety deposit box that may contain a very valuable manuscript and is going to steal it!"

Adem then gave the police directions on how to get there. "We are also on the way there," he informed the Sergeant.

Adem terminated the call. He then asked Ayesha, "So, can you please tell me what's going on?"

Ayesha quickly explained to him how she found Bilal Aksoy's hidden note inside the book of maps, and followed the clues within it to find the key in the wall of the harem at the Topkapi Palace. She then explained how she had been followed around by a male person, that their hotel room was broken into, and that finally Yavuz had lured her to the library by making her think that her friend at the library wanted to tell her something important. Meanwhile, Yavuz had been after the key that he somehow knew she had. She hadn't yet worked out how Yavuz knew that she had the key.

"So why do you want to find '*The Seven*'?" asked Adem.

"I just want to fulfil a man's last wishes," replied Ayesha. "I also think that the public should have access to the incredible beauty and knowledge contained in those manuscripts."

Adem nodded and became silent and pensive.

He continued to drive in a speedy, yet safe manner. After a few moments he spoke up. "Besides my parents, Bilal Aksoy was one of the people I most admired in this world. He took a chance on me and gave me a job when nobody else believed in me, as we were too poor for me to be able to complete a university education. He then mentored me throughout my career and even supported me to study overseas for some time. I would not be where I am today without his support and guidance."

He quickly looked in Ayesha's direction before turning back to concentrate on the road. "I'm sorry if I was abrupt the other day at the office. Yavuz Aksoy has been giving us a very hard time, sabotaging all of my decisions within the company. He was Bilal Aksoy's sole heir, but Bilal had no confidence in him. So Bilal made Yavuz's inheritance of the shares in the company dependent on Yavuz cleaning up his act. Bilal placed obligations on Yavuz to complete some education and spend significant time working within the company before he can become entitled to those shares."

Adem continued, "Of course, the things Bilal requested have not been easy for Yavuz and he is nowhere near fulfilling any of his obligations. Yavuz seems to take pleasure in making things difficult for me. In the meantime, though, I am stuck with him as it was what Bilal wanted."

"It must be unpleasant for you to see Yavuz sabotaging Bilal's company in the way he has," Ayesha commented.

"Yes it is. Yavuz had zero respect for Bilal. I could always see that, and Yavuz was always making comments about selling 'The Seven' once Bilal had passed away. It drove me mad! I tried to warn Bilal about it, but towards the end, Bilal understandably wanted peace between him and his only family and he stopped talking to me about it."

Adem continued, "So I guess when you showed up talking about *'The Seven'* it struck a nerve with me. I was worried about it all coming out into the open and that the manuscripts might be put in danger again."

"Well, it is all water under the bridge now, no worries," said Ayesha good-naturedly. "I also wrongly judged you quite harshly. I just hope we all get to the bank before Yavuz runs away with the manuscripts!"

A short time later, Adem pulled up at AKbank just as several police officers were getting out of the three police vehicles parked at the front of the bank's entrance. Ayesha could see that the police had set up a cordon surrounding the front entrance of the building. Adem went to speak to one of the officers to see what was happening. According to the officer, after Ayesha had made the call to police, they had sent out a police alert relating to Yavuz's car and number plate. A passing police patrol car had spotted Yavuz's car and followed it to the bank. Yavuz was now inside the building and police had warned the bank tellers inside that he was not to be served.

As police prepared to enter the front of the building to apprehend the suspect, Ayesha noticed a door being pushed open, close to where she was standing at the side of the building. A male figure in a blue cap emerged, looking to the right and left before sprinting out of the building and racing down the alleyway behind it. Ayesha yelled out to the police at the front of the building, "He's there! Yavuz has escaped and is heading south!"

She pointed towards the direction she had seen Yavuz run and then began running after him herself. "I can't let him get away!" she thought as she hurdled over a large piece of rubbish left in the lane. In the distance, Ayesha saw Yavuz turn left down another alleyway before she lost sight of him.

Picking up her pace, Ayesha reached the lane within a few moments. She could see that the lane ended in a dead end, which was blocked by an outside wall of a single-storey building. In the distance, Ayesha could see Berke perched up on top of the building with his hand outstretched below trying to help Yavuz scale the wall.

Ayesha saw Yavuz grab Berke's hand, but at that moment Berke lost his balance and both men tumbled back to the ground at the end of the lane. Ayesha was relieved when she saw that Yavuz did not appear to be carrying anything bulky with him. Hopefully he had not been able to obtain the manuscripts from the safety deposit box!

Ayesha yelled out, "You can't get away, Yavuz! You can't just go around assaulting people and trying to steal things!"

"Who are you to tell me what to do, you silly

little girl!" Yavuz yelled back. "Stay where you are, or you'll be sorry!"

Ayesha continued moving towards him, although she slowed down to be more cautious in her approach. She didn't want him to get away, but she knew she had to be careful for her own safety. She was about twenty metres away when she considered her next move, as she knew that the police were right behind her.

Suddenly Yavuz reached into his pocket and pulled out a small black pistol. He held it towards Ayesha and said, "I told you Miss Dean, do not come any closer...or you will be sorry!"

Ayesha stopped in her tracks when she saw the gun pointing towards her. "Oh *ya Allah*. If only I could knock it out of his hands somehow," Ayesha thought. In that instant, Ayesha heard the police behind her yelling out for Yavuz to drop the gun. Yavuz shifted his aim away from Ayesha and pointed the gun wildly in the direction of police.

She could see an expression of panic in Yavuz's eyes as he swung the gun from her to the police and back again before suddenly grabbing Berke by the neck and holding the gun to Berke's temple.

"Hey! No!" Berke said as he realised that he was now in danger of Yavuz's gun. "Please don't shoot!"

Yavuz yelled out to the police, "If you come any closer, I'll pull the trigger. Just let me get away nicely and I won't hurt anyone! I don't want to hurt anyone! Just let me go!"

By this time, a Special Forces officer had pulled Ayesha into a safer position by the side of the lane. Ayesha could hear the voice of Sergeant Omer behind her, negotiating gently with Yavuz to try to calm him down. Ayesha was impressed when it appeared that Sergeant Omer skilfully convinced Yavuz that he would have to release his hold on Berke if he wanted to climb the wall to escape.

As soon as Yavuz released the gun's aim on Berke, police shot the gun out of Yavuz's hand and efficiently apprehended both him and Berke by wrestling them both to the ground.

Ayesha allowed herself to relax as she saw the police officers restraining Yavuz in an ambulance stretcher as he was moaning and clutching at his injured hand that had been shot at by police. Some other officers accompanied Berke in handcuffs towards their police vehicle.

Ayesha stood up from her crouching position with the aid of the kind officer who had helped her to safety, straightened up her hijab, and thought, "*Alhamdulillah* everyone is safe. A long hot bath and a meat *pide* would go down really nicely right now!"

CHAPTER FIFTEEN

Ayesha, Jess and Sara were sitting on the grass in the gardens facing the Blue Mosque with Uncle Dave, Mr Isa, and Emre. They were enjoying a picnic of *pide*, doner kebab, and sweet tea. This was their second to last day in Istanbul and Ayesha could not believe that the trip would be over so soon.

After Yavuz Aksoy had been apprehended by police, Ayesha had spent the next full day tying up loose ends and assisting police in their investigation in relation to the incident. Emina had been safely found by police after Ayesha had called for her assistance, but she was a bit shaken up, with some minor scrapes and bruises. According to Emina, after Ayesha had been knocked out by Yavuz in the office, Emina had panicked and started making as much noise as she could to get help. She last saw Yavuz coming towards her with a syringe, but couldn't remember anything else. The next thing she remembered was seeing that police had arrived.

A medical check found that Emina had some of the drug Rohypnol in her system, which had the effect of impairing her memory of what had happened. She could not recall anything that had happened after she saw Ayesha getting knocked out. Thankfully, it looked like Emina would be making a full recovery. Although she was still shaken by her experience, she was grateful that both she and Ayesha had come away from the ordeal with few injuries.

The police had been overjoyed that Ayesha's

phone had recorded most of the conversation between Yavuz and Ayesha when he had kidnapped her. The police thought that the recording would provide solid evidence for the prosecution of Yavuz Aksoy. If he were to be found guilty, it would disqualify him from inheriting under Bilal Aksoy's will, as the will had a clause that would exclude Yavuz under certain circumstances including criminal activity. The inheritance would instead go towards charitable purposes.

Arslan Avci had been questioned by police on whether he had any further information in relation to the incident. Arslan stated that a few days before the kidnapping, Yavuz Aksoy had come to him demanding information about an Australian tourist named Ayesha Dean. Arslan didn't think there would be any harm in mentioning that Ayesha Dean had come to him asking about a hidden note.

But then something in Yavuz Aksoy's manner had seemed very strange to Arslan. Arslan had questioned Yavuz about why he was looking for Miss Dean, and Yavuz had told him that Ayesha had something of his that he was going to take back in whatever way necessary.

Arslan had picked up a very negative vibe from Yavuz Aksoy, so when he was in the Sultanahmet area for a delivery, Arslan had gone to the hotel to warn her. He didn't know which hotel she was staying in, but knew that it was near the Hagia Sophia. Arslan went into a few different hotels, but then gave up when he couldn't find her. Arslan thought there was only so much good he would do in one day, and his intentions were to warn Ayesha. He just didn't quite make it.

On being interviewed by police, Berke had had no qualms in pointing the finger at Yavuz Aksoy. According to Berke, when he had informed his friend Yavuz that Ayesha Dean was searching for

'The Seven', Yavuz had convinced him that 'The Seven' could once again be located as long as Berke provided him with assistance.

Being a librarian, Berke had wanted to see 'The Seven' for as long as he could remember. He told police that his greatest wish was to see 'The Seven' rightly placed in the care of the librarians who would be its guardians for the future. Berke's story was that Yavuz convinced him that Ayesha was unlawfully keeping 'The Seven' for herself, and Berke's mission was to restore 'The Seven' to its rightful place.

Ayesha laughed when Sergeant Omer recounted Berke's version of the story to her. "Oh Berke," she thought. "The creepy librarian is still on his high horse! Of course he would want to point all the blame at Yavuz when he was more than happy to lock me in a room and help Yavuz bind and gag two women! I hope he gets the justice he deserves!"

According to police, Berke also provided information relating to the break-in at Mehmet's shop, and the break-in at the hotel. Berke happily told police that Yavuz had seen Ayesha Dean standing outside his house with her friends, so Yavuz had begun following her. On one occasion he had followed her to a restaurant where he overheard her conversation and learnt that she had found a key. Yavuz told Berke of his plans to follow Ayesha to her hotel and break-in that night to steal the key. He planned to look for the key in the safe, and he had discussed with Berke various different methods of breaking into small safes.

Berke also told police that Yavuz had been worried about a dangerous gang to whom Yavuz owed a large amount of money. Yavuz had kept the gang off his back by telling them that he would soon be able to pay them from the sale of an ancient manuscript. The gang had demanded leads as to the location of the manuscript. By that stage, Yavuz had found out from Arslan that his uncle's belongings had been sold to Mehmet's shop. Unfortunately for Mehmet, the shop had been ransacked by some of the gang members who were impatient and thought they could find clues to the location of the manuscript themselves.

Ayesha was brought back to the present when she heard Sara let out a loud sigh of contentment as she bit into a succulent piece of Turkish delight. Attempting to wipe the sugar from her lips, and with her mouth still half full, Sara asked, "So Ayesha, can you please explain to us again how you managed to become a matchmaker on this trip along with solving a hundred-year-old mystery about the location of a famous manuscript?"

Ayesha laughed, "You know I never mean to be the matchmaker! Opportunities just somehow fall into my lap!"

"What happened?" Emre asked in an interested manner.

"Emre, if you're planning on remaining a bachelor," warned Uncle Dave, "Don't get in the way of Ayesha Dean. She has a host of friends from which she is bound to find the perfect match for you…and to Ayesha's credit, they usually work out!"

"Day! No, don't say that, it's embarrassing! Sorry Emre, please ignore him," Ayesha chided Uncle Dave as Emre smiled and lowered his eyes. Uncle Dave grinned. He enjoyed keeping Ayesha's potential suitors on their toes. Ayesha was as close to him as a daughter and he knew that whomever Ayesha eventually chose to marry would need to possess good character and integrity. Any suitor with half a chance would need to be able to withstand a little ribbing from Uncle Dave!

Ayesha began her explanation of what had happened after Yavuz and Berke had been apprehended by police. "Well, after Yavuz was arrested, the police recovered the key, along with my bracelet." Ayesha happily held her wrist up to show the others that her bracelet had been returned.

"I then met up with Adem Demir and we went into the bank. As Mr Demir was the executor of Bilal Aksoy's will, he was able to access the safety deposit box and guess what we found?"

"You found *'The Seven'*?" Emre asked happily.

"Yes! It was wrapped up in several scrolls and we didn't want to damage the manuscripts, so Mr Demir and I took them to the library straight away. Adem Demir had known for a long time that it was Bilal Aksoy's wish for *'The Seven'* to be properly preserved and he was happy to deal with all the paperwork for the transfer of the manuscripts to the library's care."

Ayesha continued, "Anyway, when we got to

the library, poor Emina was in a stretcher and they were taking her to hospital to be treated. Mr Demir felt so bad that Yavuz Aksoy had caused all this trouble, so he's been visiting the library every day since the incident to see how Emina is doing."

"How is she doing?" Jess asked.

"Emina is fine, just a few bruises and scrapes. I think the fact that Mr Demir is visiting her everyday has made her completely forget about the discomfort! She thinks he may be 'The One' and he looks completely smitten when they're together!" Ayesha said happily.

Sara laughed, "Ayesha Dean the matchmaker does it again!"

Ayesha smiled, "Well, I don't think I had much to do with it! Anyway, you can all see the happy couple for yourselves. I've arranged with Emina for us to view the manuscripts in their new display at the Suleymaniye Library today!"

***

Later that day, Ayesha and her friends visited the Suleymaniye Library. Ayesha felt a little sad that the trip was coming to an end, but she was hopeful that this would not be the last time she would visit Istanbul.

As a radiant Emina and Adem led the group of travellers to the special display cabinet in the library's show room, Emre took the chance to speak with Ayesha. "I hope this isn't the end of our friendship, Ayesha," he smiled. "You'll come back again one day soon, won't you?"

Ayesha grinned happily. "Of course I would love to come back one day," she smiled. "Hopefully sooner rather than later."

By this time the group had reached the impressive display that Emina had requested her staff to put together. The room was dimly lit to help preserve the ancient manuscripts on display. In pristine glass display cabinets, Emina's staff had arranged Ibn Arabi's *Awrad al-Usbu, The Seven Days of the Heart*, in glass frames to support the fragile paper.

Ayesha thought the manuscripts were breathtakingly beautiful with swirling patterns of gold leaf and striking colours surrounding the numerous pages of Arabic script. Emina was making arrangements for a skilled calligrapher to beautifully scribe English and Turkish translations of the *Awrad* for the display. In the meantime, the typed translations were displayed underneath each page of the ancient manuscript.

Adem caught Ayesha's eye and said, "I want to formally thank you for everything you have done to fulfil Bilal Aksoy's dying wish. *InshAllah* he is now at peace. I'm very grateful that '*The Seven*' are in their rightful place."

He then smiled, "I also have you to thank for bringing me to Emina. You'll be very pleased to know my parents are extremely happy that my bachelorhood may soon be coming to an end."

Ayesha exclaimed, "That is the best news! I am so happy for all of you!"

Ayesha's heart filled with happiness and satisfaction. "*Alhamdulillah*! What a trip! I can't wait for the next one, *inshAllah*!" she thought as she turned towards the display to keep reading one of her favourite passages from the *Awrad-al-Usbu*.

"I ask of You, O Allah, that I may flee from me to You and that my whole totality may be integrated in You, so that the sense of my existence ceases to veil me from my witnessing.

O You who are my aim and aspiration, O You whom I worship and adore!

Nothing is lost to me when I have found You! Nothing is unknown to me when I have known You! Nothing is missing from me when I have witnessed You!

My annihilation is in You; My subsistence is through You; and You are the object of my contemplation.

There is no god but You, as You have attested, as you have known, and as You have ordered."

ACKNOWLEDGEMENTS

In the Name of Allah, the Most Merciful, the Most Compassionate. I'd firstly like to acknowledge that the final quotation in this story is taken from a beautiful translation of "The Sunday Morning Prayer", **The Seven Days of the Heart, by Ibn Arabi,** translated in English by Pablo Beneito and Stephen Hirtenstein, (2000), by Anqa Publishing, United Kingdom.

Special thanks to the following people whose advice, assistance and support played an invaluable part in bringing this Ayesha Dean story to life…My beloved siblings Imran and Marryam Lum, and my beautiful sister-in-law Anisa Buckley for all the brainstorming, editing, proofreading, suggestions and support. Koel Rizer, for the laughs, and hours spent discussing the difference between Australian versus American language. My editor, Helen Koehne, who helped me to see the wood for the trees, and skilfully made everything sound better! Nuri Septina for the gorgeous cover illustration and design. My parents, for providing love and inspiration, and for being my "go-to" source for anything related to Ibn Arabi. Finally, my favourite boys in the world, my husband James and son Ilyaas, for being totally awesome.

Stay tuned for the next Ayesha Dean adventure COMING SOON!

Register at www.melatilum.com.au for updates and news on competitions, events, and releases!

If you enjoyed this Ayesha Dean adventure please kindly leave a review at www.amazon.com and www.goodreads.com

Follow Melati on:

Facebook: Melati Lum Author
Instagram: Melati.lum
Twitter: @Melatilum

CPSIA information can be obtained
at www.ICGtesting.com
Printed in the USA
LVHW011702160119
604152LV00003B/650/P

9 780994 460509